In the Gathering Woods

Drue Heinz Literature Prize 2000

In the Gathering Woods

ADRIA BERNARDI

To Jeannine
with best wishes
to a fabulous storyteller —
at Bend
Nov. 9, 2006

University of Pittsburgh Press

Manufactured in the United States of America

Printed on acid-free paper

10 9 8 7 6 5 4 3 2 1

Acknowledgments will be found at the end of the book.

ISBN 0-8229-5782-5

To Jeffrey Stovall

Contents

In the Gathering Woods

In the Gathering Woods

I t seemed that I had waited many years before my grandfather, Isaia, asked me to accompany him on his forays, and finally, when I was seven years old, he said to my mother, I think it is time you let the boy come with me.

How they unfolded before me, each taking its place in my mind, I learned from him. Each family, each category. He showed me their habitats, which ones grew in pastures, dead wood, dung. I learned from him how each fell into one of three categories: edible, toxic, mortal. During those many outings, it seemed impossible to me that I would ever know with certainty. How could I be trusted to know the difference between the *prugnolo* and the deadly *tignosa bianca*, both blindingly white? Those that were safe were frequently revolting in appearance, while the benign-looking often proved deadly.

I was a quiet child, with narrow shoulders, slender limbs, serious and withdrawn, who, beneath a polite, reserved self, had always been wildly fascinated with fright. Alone for hours on end in the fields, I would contrive tales and could, with a detailed telling, scare myself, take myself to the edge of a precipice, always able at the last minute to yank myself back and resume my task as if I had never summoned up the fear, simply whistle for the dog and begin to round up the sheep again. I drew from an ample well of stories, having heard of ravens who plucked shepherds out of pastures, of innkeepers who killed guests and served them for dinner to pilgrims travelling through. But during that year when I began to learn the nature of mushrooms from my grandfather Isaia, I stopped the game of deliberately scaring myself, no longer certain I could check fright at will; increasingly, I became consumed with fear, suffering often from episodes of panic, terrified that I would make a fatal mistake and be responsible for the careless oversight that resulted in the poisoning of my entire family.

Early that October morning when Isaia first took me out, he shook my shoulder, waking me. He said in a whisper like far-off thunder, *Indemma*. Let's go. Instantaneously, I became alert and dressed myself quickly, the stone floor cold against my soles.

It was dark when we left Tavolanuda, each carrying a weathered basket. Fog obscured all but the closest trees. We walked on the via Giardini past Casacinque, through the hamlet of Barigelli. We turned onto a mountain path called Pianaccio Fiammineda, flaming path. We walked for several hours and met no one.

As we approached a thick forest of pine trees, Isaia said: This is where we leave the path. With his right hand, he grabbed the trunk of a tree above and hoisted himself up. He scaled the mountainside with ease, reaching from tree to tree, using each to pull himself higher up the slope, while I, on my knees, grasped at low bushes and saplings to keep from falling backwards. He waited above at a level place. When I reached him, I was out of breath and he was on his haunches calmly cutting a mushroom at the base of its stem.

Look at its shape, Costante, he said to me. A true mushroom shape: the cap, like a broad, flattened dome; the stem, thick and smooth.

Boleto granuloso.

Look at the parts. The cap is covered with a film, not dry. Look at the particles on the stem, which are grainy.

As he cut and gathered more mushrooms, he seemed to pay no attention to me. I moved quickly, hopping from place to place in order to quickly fill my basket.

Isaia stopped me. Do not be in too much of a rush; that is how mistakes are made.

When my grandfather finished gathering the mushrooms, he waved for me to follow him back to the path.

As we walked along, I heard only our footsteps, Isaia's long strides settling loudly into his heavy boots, mine clicking lightly, unevenly, upon the stones of the path. I wore a new pair of wooden shoes, *zoccoli,* and my soles slipped against the slick carpet of moss and lichen. I slipped frequently. I veered from left to right on the path, peering into the woods above and below but not daring to enter. I lagged farther and farther behind my grandfather, looking into the dense layers of limbs, tempting pricks of uneasiness, hoping to see an animal move. Perhaps a hare. Or a boar, the *cinghiale,* a powerful, horrible beast with its snout rooting in the soil.

Isaia followed the path around a bend to the left, and by not following him I permitted him to disappear. I was alone. I stood still in my fear, able to run after him, but unwilling. I preferred to remain there, an epicenter separate within a sphere of fog. The fog caressed my face with a cool dampness, surrounding me, isolating me. Suddenly, it gripped my throat and I could barely breathe. From my throat, there rose to my ears, a quick-throbbing, murmuring thud, my heart beating so rapidly that I was unable to move, the fog so close I could not see. I was lost to the trees.

And there, in a tangle of branches entwined in a crushing dependency, I saw them for the first time, the Ugly Children, their bulging eyes accusing me. Their shrill voices called out, *Guarzetto!* Hey, boy! they called to me again and again. Hey boy! I can still hear the dissonant staccato as they shrieked, *zetto, zetto, zetto!* like giant, evil insects.

I ran from them, the soles of my wooden shoes slipping on the rocks, seeing nothing but a blur of grey ahead and charred limbs reaching from either side. I ran on a path I could not see, to a point I could not find.

Costante!

At last, I heard my name. My grandfather sounded as if he had entered the valley below us. I ran until I saw his white hair bristling beneath the edge of his cap.

Our land was on an east-facing slope, one of the few farms with a flat expanse for pastures and fields. Above, on the culm of the slope, there was once a fine stand of chestnut trees. Our household consisted of my grandfather, my grandmother, my mother, and myself. My father, a stonecutter, had gone to quarry in Corsica and died in an explosion when I was still an infant.

Our farm was called Tavolanuda and had been in our family since my grandfather's grandfather married the only daughter of a prosperous shepherd. He came to own thirty hectares of land at a time when most others owned only five. His prosperity did not succeed him, however, and neither of his two sons achieved the station he had envisioned for them.

My great-great-grandfather, for whom my grandfather was named, dreamed that his first-born son, Orazio, would become a scholar and go down to the plains, to Modena, to teach classics. Instead, Orazio heard the voice of God at an early age and entered the seminary at Fiumalbo. He willed fifteen hectares, his entire birthright, to the Church, in whose hands the land has remained to this day, untouched, unused. The other son was named Napoleone Bonaparte. My grandfather's grandfather was a great supporter of France and of French culture; he wished for his son to be a leader of free men, but Bonaparte was not. After serving in the army for twelve years, he returned to Tavolanuda and continued to play the *cavaliere*, having grown accustomed to the privileges of a low-ranking officer. While his father was alive, Bonaparte's gambling debts were manageable, eventually recouped in subsequent games or with his father's assistance. With the death of Isaia, however, there was no longer a harness, and the debts accumulated until they threatened the welfare of the family. Little by little, Bonaparte sold off the chestnut trees from the property above, until it was completely deforested. It is from this point in time that the farm became known as Tavolanuda, the naked table.

After denuding the land, Bonaparte nearly succeeded in losing what remained. Besieged by friends and acquaintances to whom he owed money, he sold off seven hectares. For a pittance, he sold off the crest of the hill where the chestnut trees had once stood. Then, in order to pay off the remaining debt, he took a loan from a man named Orlandini who came from La Rocca. That village sat on an enormous rock, its houses, were made of slate-colored stone. Behind it loomed

Sasso Tignoso, a bare mountain peak, whose name signifies "nasty and mean." The people of La Rocca had a reputation for stinginess and for avarice, and it was said that the infants there suckled, not at the breasts of their mothers, but on rocks, nourished only by dew.

Orlandini, the man to whom my great-grandfather owed money, had made a modest fortune with his flock of sheep. His commercial success earned him a reputation as the local moneylender, and, for this, he was excommunicated. Orlandini's younger brother had served in the cavalry with Bonaparte, and so he took pity and bought off Bonaparte's remaining debt for a modest rate of interest. Over the years, the debt remained and interest accrued. With Bonaparte having no timber left to sell, and making no move to repay the debt, Orlandini called in his loan.

The night Bonaparte attempted to win back his losses, the stakes were very high. In a game of *briscola,* he bet the land against a man from Buccoterra whose name was Brut'figlioli. My great-grandfather lost one tract of land, then two, then all eight remaining hectares. On the last hand, his rival thumped down the three of spades, the trump, a *briscola.* He had lost the house itself.

Bonaparte challenged Brut'figlioli to another game.

Ma cos'ad ghè a scommar'? What do you have left to bet? he asked. The land was gone, the house.

Me fiô, Bonaparte said to him across the table. My son. And that way if I lose, you'll have one good-looking heir.

The men crowding around that table were with my great-grandfather. Not that they cared for him, they didn't; he was arrogant and had soft hands.

But Brut'figlioli, they despised, for it was said, he had begotten the ugliest children that God had ever created. They had wild hair, knotted and twisted like mildewed rope into hideous snake curls, and their eyes protruded from the sockets. They resembled insects and spoke in shrill, incomprehensible voices. They were, it was said, conceived in the womb of a gypsy by the seed of a bedouin. These were the children known as the Ugly Children, the very ones who called out to me in the forest, the very ones whose piercing shrieks had sent me running toward my grandfather. It was to the Brut'figlioli family that my great-grandfather had risked losing his son.

At midnight, Bonaparte said to Brut'figlioli, And now we'll change the game. I want to play *scopa*.

Brut'figlioli agreed and Bonaparte wagered his son. They played only one game.

All the cards fell to Bonaparte, and some took it as proof that the Lord blesses those who remember the Church in their offerings. It was said that Orazio, by this time at a monastery in Ferrara, had heard the prayers of his brother, and that he had prayed. O heavenly Lord, as I have offered Thee already my entire earthly estate, please look with favor upon my brother Napoleone Bonaparte in this his hour of need. It was said that he prayed in Latin and that then he prayed in the language of the mountains. *Aiutatelu che gioga ben'.* Help him to play well.

Bonaparte, who had bet his son for the return of the house and the land, won in three hands, sweeping up each time the *set' bello,* the majority of diamonds, the majority of the cards, the queen and a *scopa.* In only one hand did Brut'figlioli win a single point, the unenviable point, for taking the sixes and sevens. With three *scope* in his hands, Tavolanuda and the child were his again. On the day he won back

Tavolanuda, my great-grandfather gave up gambling and turned his attention to the land, and my grandfather grew up knowing how to cultivate and how to read.

⁂

In our mountains, the snow fell from October until April, and those too weak to push open the doors jammed shut by snowdrifts were known to have died of starvation inside their homes. It was a lonely time at Tavolanuda, and during the winter, we desperately anticipated the voices of the men who had been hired by the road supervisor, the *cantoniere*, to clear the snow. As they neared from the direction of the house called Campanile, we would first hear a gravelly hum, which grew gradually louder. Then we would hear the scraping of shovels, the tromping of boots, and, when they were upon us, the squeaking of snow and ice beneath their soles.

They were led in song by a man named 'Cello, christened Marcello, nicknamed Violoncello, because the pitch and depth of his voice were as precise and as stirring as that instrument when it is finely tuned.

Heard perhaps four or five times a season, 'Cello's voice infused hope, and his song helped break the monotony of our muffled silence. In winter, these men were one of the few reminders that others inhabited the universe.

He would sing and call, *Un mazzolin' di fiori.* A little bouquet of flowers.

And the gang would answer, *Che vien' de' la montagna.* That comes from the mountains.

My mother Beatrice allowed me to stand in the doorway and watch and listen. She even allowed herself, a widow, to stand in the doorway to hear better. But she would not allow me beyond the threshold because, she said, the men were atheists and used foul language. I stood with my back against the wooden door, looking at the road and, across it, at the mountain wall, which was a dazzling white, triumphantly emerged for a moment from the clouds that had locked it away for days on end within an ashen chaos. I would wait and watch as this gang of twenty men neared, each man built like a mule, flinging shovels full of snow, clearing a path so that people could travel until the next snowstorm. This was the road that the emigrants travelled each autumn, the charcoalmakers and the wet nurses and the shepherds and the stoneworkers like my father, who went down out of the mountains. They went far away and many houses were left empty. But we remained in our house and were comforted by the sight of this benevolent swarm, a mist of white surrounding it. We were consoled by the sound of its merciful humming, as it moved slowly up the road toward our house, swelling as it neared us, then dissipating as the last man rounded the bend and disappeared in the direction of Serpiano.

Like spring, my birth was eagerly awaited, and I was welcomed with relief. I remained for the old people a perpetual reassurance that endurance would be rewarded with survival. The spring of my eighth birthday followed an exceptionally long winter. When my birthday arrived that year, the feast day of San Bernardino at the end of May, I was to accompany Isaia again on one of his outings; this time, however, he did not need to shake me awake, for I was already dressed and sitting downstairs on the wooden chair beside the door when he came down the granite steps.

As we walked, I peered into the dark, trying to guess where he was taking me. For a kilometer, he said not one word. The main road curved to the left, and we followed a footpath to the right which descended gently. As we walked among the scattered trees, the sun's fingertips emerged across the valley from behind the mountain called Cimone, and by the time we had crossed through the thin woods, it was daylight. My grandfather pointed to a pile of rocks at the edge of a field, a *mas'rin,* it was called, a mound of stones made by the women and children who had cleared the field. We sat down on this heap, and ate our breakfast of bread and cheese and onion.

Eat a mushroom only if its identity is certain.

With his pocketknife he cut a piece of bread and handed it to me.

If you have a speck of doubt, my grandfather said, leave it alone. Only ask the opinion of someone you trust.

I absorbed his warnings through my skin. I had heard from my schoolmates about a family from beyond Piandelagotti that had been killed years ago by ingesting poisonous mushrooms.

The boy had been whipped by his father for losing one of the sheep. To get back into his father's good graces, he arose early one morning and went to a faraway field to collect mushrooms. He gathered dozens of deadly mushrooms, mistaking them for a similar-looking white mushroom called the *prataliolo,* which is benign. When he returned home, the father was skeptical, but relented because the boy was so confident and convincing in his argument. The mother cooked the mushrooms in butter and garlic that evening. The next morning they were all dead, even the old grandfather.

After we finished our morning meal, we started walking again, continuing another half-kilometer along the edge of the field. There, in the grass, was an expanse of little sponge-like creatures. Isaia bent down over the mushrooms, squatting, with an elbow resting on his knee.

Look at the stem, child.

It was thick and white

Do you know the butcher Mazzinelli? Do you know his hands?

I did. Who could forget the hands of that man? Broad, with short thick fingers, wider at the nail.

Think of his thumb and you will remember this stem, Isaia said. The top of this mushroom is a yellowish brown, round like the sponges the Fontana brothers bring back each season from Sardegna.

That day I learned to identify the *spugnola gialla*. The thick-stemmed morel. There is nothing else that resembles it, Isaia said, nothing edible or toxic or deadly. If you see it once, you will remember it forever.

In teaching me about the mushrooms, Isaia selected as his earliest examples the edible mushrooms that are most easily identified.

When we had filled my grandfather's basket, he said, *Ora turnemmo in dré*. We'll go back now.

That evening for my birthday, we feasted on those mushrooms and roasted hare.

One Sunday, in July of that year, Isaia excused me from Mass. When we started out, it was cool, but the clear sky promised that the day would be hot. We walked through town, through Ardonlà, through the piazza and under the arch of the wall. Then we followed a footpath up the hill behind the town.

Green, damp grass covered the mountainside, and everywhere I looked, I could see mushrooms.

Here? I asked.

No. Not yet, he said.

But look, I said, all of these mushrooms, right here in front of us.

Quiet, child, quiet, my grandfather said. Walk. These are not the mushrooms we want.

I wanted to talk.

I was filled with the optimism inspired by a Sunday morning in summer before others are out and about. I talked at great length about nothing in particular, my grandfather saying nothing, except, once in awhile, I see.

As we walked along a narrow ledge on the slope, the sun warmed our backs. As we got closer to the top of the hill, there were meadows, with no trees, except for a lone chestnut tree. We passed the tree, then began our final ascent. When I felt gravity pulling my legs faster and faster down the hill, I knew we were on a new face, overlooking a valley, looking south and west.

Do you want to see Pisa? Isaia asked me.

Yes, yes.

My grandfather cupped his hands beneath my jaw and chin, pointing me outward. I put my hands over his hands and held on, pulling my legs up under me; he lifted me up to his level, and said, Do you see Pisa?

Yes, yes, It's there. There. I see the Tower falling to the ground.

Do you see Lucca?

Yes, yes, I see Lucca, too. I see the cathedral and the old city wall.

It was a familiar game, one we had played many times when I was younger but one played infrequently now that I had grown older.

And do you see Modena, too?

No, no, I answered quickly. I had played too many times to be fooled. Modena is in the other direction, to the north.

So you haven't forgotten, Isaia said, easing me back to the ground. Now, Costante, he said, look around you.

I stood in the center of a tremendous circle of mushrooms that were the color of butter and cream, backlit by the early-morning sun. I was ringed by fairies with spindly legs, their heads covered by the wide hats of rich ladies, faces hidden, nodding to one another, brims touching gently as they laughed and danced around me.

I could barely absorb what I was seeing. Gossiping fairies, waving bonnets. My legs tingled. I wanted to stand there forever.

These mushrooms, my grandfather said as he grabbed my hand and led me outside the circle, grow in a circle like this. No one knows why.

These mushrooms are called *gambe secche.*

I was hardly listening. I did not want Isaia's words to interrupt the moment, but the lightness of the other world was fleeting, dissipating into an ever-widening circle, thinning until it dissolved into a meadow of harsh rays.

Are you listening? What are they called?

Gambe secche.

When I spoke, the last thread snapped, the circle disappeared, and I stood in the meadow squinting.

Why are they called by that name? my grandfather asked.

Because the legs are thin and long and dry, I answered.

We bent over to collect the mushrooms and Isaia explained how their caps are shaped like domes, with edges that are upturned. Their color is light brown, sometimes whitish. Underneath, it is like a fan, the gills are separated and wide. But it is the legs, he said, remember the legs, they are tall and thin, a dull color. The stem looks as if it can hardly support the cap.

The day was already hot when we were done filling our baskets and Isaia announced we would return home. We headed back up the hill, retracing our steps. I said nothing, trying to remember the way the fairies had looked, the nodding brims of their hats.

This time when we passed the lone chestnut tree, we saw our neighbor, Gambetto, sitting against the trunk drinking from a bottle of wine.

Eh, Isaia. He called to us as we approached.

Gambetto. My grandfather calmly answered.

Ma cos'ad ghè? he asked my grandfather, pointing to the basket. What have you got there? Mushrooms?

My grandfather did not answer his question. Instead, he asked Gambetto what he was doing there on a Sunday morning. *Ma cos'ad fa qui 'sta menga matin'?*

I'm drinking. What does it look like I'm doing?

His eyes were a crystal blue covered with film. He squinted at us from beneath the bill of his cap.

Ne voi un guccin'? A drop? he said, handing my grandfather the bottle.

No, Isaia said. Woe to those who are heroes at drinking.

Ad ga ragión. You're right, he said.

Have you heard? Gambetto asked.

Heard?

Le roi est morte.

What?

The king is dead.

He took a drink.

In Monza.

He took another drink.

Killed by a weaver from Prato.

And now, they will demand that we poor peasants grieve for the monarchy, Gambetto said.

Sè, sè, Isaia said. Yes yes.

Parce que le roi le dit, Gambetto said, his index finger stabbing the air. Because the king says so.

Are you sure you don't want a drink? Gambetto asked again.

We're late enough already, Isaia said. We're going home. The wife and daughter will get me good if we are gone much longer.

Women! Gambetto said, his face beardless, unshaven, in the modern fashion.

Dov'è il giudizio delle donne? he demanded of me. Where do women keep common sense?

I shrugged, squirmed, uncomfortable in my ignorance.

Sotto le scarpe! he said. Beneath the soles of their shoes! That's where their common sense is.

I looked for my grandfather to contradict him. To say, No, women have good common sense and use it. To say, Who else does all the work when the men go away? But he did not and only shook his head.

We parted, leaving Gambetto with his back against the tree, his long, spindly legs extended casually upon the ground.

Autumn was late that year, and at the end of September, the leaves had not yet begun to turn; October belonged to neither summer nor fall, and we enjoyed the weather uneasily, as if too much comfort would bring about a change. It was during this time that my episodes of panic increased both in frequency and in intensity, but I kept the fears to myself, and if my grandfather and my mother suspected, they did not speak of it to me.

During that season, I was introduced to many mushrooms, including the *Amanitae,* a family that includes the most deadly mushrooms, as well some that are succulent and benign. In our mountains, the *ovulo buono* was a prized mushroom. Like the location of buried treasure, its hiding places were guarded family secrets. Often, the youngest child was assigned to the rear of the gathering party for the purpose of reporting if it was being followed. Like the child-partisans in the war of my middle years, children were given the responsibility of deciding whether to divert the spy or race ahead and warn the others of impending danger.

The *ovulo buono* was coveted by the ancient Romans, including the Emperor Caesar; its scientific name, *Amanita caesara*, is derived from his name. Its cap, which ranges in color from deep red to orange, fades to amber with age. Were it not for their desire to keep secret the sacred location, gatherers would howl with abandon as they collected them and put them into their baskets.

But to this day, I cannot join in this jubilation. The *Amanitae*, whether poisonous or benign, push forth from a sac, like a prehistoric reptile from a mucous egg; this emergence, neither animal-birth nor vegetable-sprouting, repulsed me. Were it not for the *Amanita* family, I might have made a respectable biologist. As it was, I retreated to the smaller, neater abstractions of chemical bonds.

It was that autumn, during a gathering at my aunt's house for a cousin's baptism, when I first heard of the *Amanitae* that were deadly.

I sat in the corner, next to the fireplace. The adults sat at the table, drinking a bitter liqueur distilled from cherries, a coveted treat, but one which I would never learn to like. The mother-in-law of my Zia Albertina, my father's sister, told the story. I had never liked being near the old woman, whose name was Filomena. Her hands were like claws and she constantly grabbed my hand or arm, poisoning me with her staleness. Now that I am an old man, I can see that her grip was a desperate plea, and I, too, have sensed the revulsion with which the young often greet my touch; a few short years ago this was not the case, but now it is so.

Filomena sat, as she always did, at the middle of the table, her back to the fireplace and in profile to me. She told of a boy, from the house named Mattoni, who had died. He was exactly your age, she said, pointing to me.

How could the child have known? Filomena began, a scarf cutting a horizon above her eyebrows. He had eaten the *tignosa verdognola* one afternoon. And in three days.

In tre dí.

He was dead.

L'era mort'.

What happened? What happened? the adults asked her, each moving his chair closer. They leaned toward her, perched. They spoke in the quickened phrases and hushed tones of mock-dread that signified their attentive attraction to the horror.

My mother quickly looked at me in the corner, but I did not look at her, knowing that if she caught my eye, she would banish me to a bedroom upstairs and I would miss hearing Filomena's story. Instead, I gazed at the fire, feigning absorption in the flames and pretending to be oblivious to the conversation of the adults. I was certain she would have sent me upstairs, up those narrow steps with a rope for a railing; but she was distracted from making a decision when Filomena continued speaking.

Son' ignoranti, lor'li di Mattoni, she said. They are stupid, heads of brick, the ones who live at Mattoni, just like the name of their house. Nobody told the poor boy. The green mushroom is dangerous. It kills. Yet no one told him. No one. And now, he is dead.

The crooked tips of her index fingers rested upon the edge of the table. She lifted her hands slowly for emphasis.

The boy was out with his sister, she said, while they were watching the sheep. They were hungry and hot and went into a forest at the edge of the pasture to have something to eat. This is what the girl says. This is as she described it.

This boy, a blusterer like his father and his father before him, said to the sister: How is a man supposed to get strength from a sliver of cheese and stale tree-bread?

And he got up. He tromped into the woods and the sister followed him.

Here, he said. Here. He bent over and cut three mushrooms.

The sister said nothing because she was afraid of contradicting her brother. The boy held the mushroom up over his head, imitating his father, saying, The meat of the gods, the meat of the gods. With the corner of his shirt, he wiped the dirt from the mushrooms.

The girl said, I have never seen a mushroom like that at our table.

He called her a little fool. What do you know? Women are good only for having babies. Stupid. Like the sheep. Common sense on the bottom of their shoes.

Afraid of his anger, the sister said no more, relieved when he put the mushroom into a pouch that hung from his belt.

Filomena raised the crooked index finger of her left hand. After a couple of hours, the boy complained of hunger and turned on his sister: Why are you hiding food from me?

She said that this was not true. That they had eaten all the food they were given. She told him to not be mean.

Mean? he said. Never. I have mushrooms and I am going to eat all of them.

And with that, he bit into the cap of one of the mushrooms he had picked.

Every one of you sitting here around this table knows what the *tignosa verdognola* looks like. It looks like a spring day. The color of new grass, the sweet young leaves of lettuce. He did not know. He thought he had picked the *colombina verde*. He did not know anything.

He bit into it. Bitter! He threw away the rest of the mushroom along with the two others.

At first, the sister was calmed, but when they approached the house and crossed the threshing floor, she was filled with dread.

That night, just before the family went to bed, the boy fell from his chair, clutching his stomach. On the cold stone floor, he cried out, vomiting and begging for water. Water! Water! His thirst was so great.

The sister called out that he had eaten a mushroom, that she had said not to, but that he had.

The father, ignorant, always ignorant, called to his wife to get the boy some wine to kill the poison.

He carried that boy to a bed upstairs. So much pain, so much pain, that his face, so beautifully round and rosy a few hours ago, was now shrunken like a prune and the color of a bruise. For two days, he suffered attacks in the stomach, the liver, and his face turned from purple to yellow. In two days he was like an old man. He fell asleep and never woke up.

When she concluded, the adults shook their heads, looking down, saying, Poor child.

Isaia was unmoved. He did not join the others as they silently shook their heads. He was hard in his lack of sympathy.

Had someone taken the time to instruct the boy, Isaia said, he would be alive. The *colombina verde* does not grow this time of year and his father, so quick to grab a bottle of wine, sealed the fate of his son. Alcohol spreads poison through the blood. There are some deaths that cannot be avoided, the deaths of pestilence and war, but he died a stupid death.

This story was alive in my mind that autumn morning when my grandfather and I made another foray, this time up the main road toward Abetone, a town on the border between of our province and Toscana. I no longer wanted to learn about these plants. As we passed Fiumalbo, my grandfather told me that there are people who will say they have sure ways to distinguish mushrooms, who know shortcuts and easy ways to learn. For example, they will say that if you are able to peel the skin from the cap, it is an edible mushroom. But this is not true: you can peel off the layer of the *ovulo malefico,* which is poisonous, just as easily you can the meadow mushroom. Others will say that if you cook a mushroom, you cook the poison juices out. False, he said. False. Some men claim that poisonous mushrooms will cause silver to turn black, and that if a mushroom does not, it is therefore safe. False. And fools are frequently adamant.

Isaia grabbed my wrist and pulled me into the woods beside the road.

On this elm tree, look, he said, pointing to indigo-tinted mushrooms.

They look like ears, I said.

These mushrooms were named *orrechione.* Big ears. Their undersides were fanned.

We walked a few feet deeper into the woods.

Once, Isaia said, I heard a man claim that if you find a stretch of edible mushrooms, you are safe because the poisonous and edible do not inhabit the same places.

He pointed to an oak, showing me the a deadly *Amanita,* one which in our region was called the *tignosa di primavera.* Spring's nasty one. The English call it the destroying angel.

Life and death are here next to one another, he said to me. Had the boy from Mattoni, so headstrong, so impatient, only turned around and picked this one, he would be living.

Smell it, Isaia directed.

It smelled like a cellar, like the cantina where we stored potatoes and onions, chestnut flour and cornmeal, for the winter.

On the left, at the base of the trees, he pointed to another mushroom.

Its cap was bright red and covered with white flecks. I had no clue. It could assuage hunger or it could kill me. The warts repulsed me but the color was pleasing. Its stem was thick. It emerged from a sac at its base. Just ahead on the ground was a similar mushroom, this one the color of rust, its cap also covered with flecks.

My grandfather said nothing as I looked at the spotted mushrooms before me, unable to distinguish one from another, seeing everywhere I looked in the woods, mushrooms emerging, strange organisms, passive, taunting. Still my grandfather said nothing. Did he want me to attempt an observation? Did he want me to remain silent? I stared at the second spotted mushroom, struggling to identify its character. My face felt flushed. My heartbeat accelerated. Did one look like the other? It seemed that mushrooms all over the woods leaned toward me, demanding an answer, a correct answer. I heard in my head: Stupid, stupid, stupid. You will never know.

I did not move for many minutes and from inside the din, I heard Isaia's muffled voice edging between me and my taunters. He recited a lesson I could not hear, but I recognized his solemn drone and was able to discern certain words between my heartbeats.

Both were toxic. The *Amanita muscaria* and the *Amanita pantherina*. Two of the most deadly mushrooms. As I walked home with Isaia, I resolved to learn no more, because every time I learned something new, it seemed fraught with ambiguity, and so much of what seemed uncertain was dangerous as well.

They were always out there. In my mind, in this period of my young life, the Ugly Children were always out there, the ill-begotten offspring of Brut'figlioli. They lived, high, high up, and no one had ever seen them. They were locked up in his house, never coming to school because, I believed, they were too grotesque, too deformed to stand with us as we said our prayers. Beggars and merchants avoided the house of Brut'figlioli. And he kept them in the house all the time, ashamed of his own flesh and blood. How many of them were there? It was said there were as many as thirty and as few as three. No one knew for certain, because Brut'figlioli never let them out. It was only at night, when he slept in his drunken stupor, that they emerged from their house and spied upon us. The Ugly Children never separated from one another, travelling together in a swarm, like insects in the night. Lying awake in bed, I could imagine their voices, shrieking chirps intermingled with the night's grating chorus.

In early October of that same year, one mid-afternoon, I was working in a far pasture with a scythe, and it became unbearably hot. Hearing the water down below in the river Scoltenna, I decided to go down the steep, wooded slope, and I emerged scratched by briers and thorns. I chose a flat rock at the water's edge and I sat there lost in thought, wondering about nature, about how things were made: How did clouds, which have weight, stay afloat? How could water stay together in a drop yet break apart into smaller particles? Suddenly, it became very dark. It was as if a purple cape had been draped over me, gripping my shoulders, smothering me. I could not manage a true breath and inhaled shallow, uneven gulps of the humid river air. Heat clung to me, like the air suspended between a face and a mask. I pulled my knees to my chest, making myself smaller, as if by leaning to one side of the rock or another I would drop into an abyss. I closed my eyes tightly, afraid to look behind me into the woods or up at the blackened sky or down at the river. I was the center point in a vacuum of silence. No leaf moved. And though my eyes were closed, locked shut against the world, my ears were funnels waiting for a sound.

A lone insect cried. A tickling vibrato pierced the silence. Two leaves of a bush behind me began to rub against one another. This rustling rose up higher, up to the top of the tallest tree, becoming an insect wail. The voice called *'zetto! zitto! 'zetto!* Hey boy, the wail said, Be quiet. It begged silence of me, me who was retracted and silent, except for the chaotic pounding inside my chest.

The solitary insect voice was joined by others. *Zitto, zitto!* There was an expanding din behind my ears, above me. I could feel the insects nearing my face, brushing against my cheeks, but I refused to open my eyes. They did not alight on my face, but hummed near me. I swatted the air, but still they continued. They encircled me, then retreated. I hid my face in my arms, my ears were assaulted as they taunted me, Open your eyes, boy, open your eyes.

I covered my eyes with my hands; my hands were sweaty and tingling. They did not feel like my hands. Was it my face? Were they my hands? They were incompatible, as if hands and face belonged to two separate creatures, as if I were experiencing the touch of my face as another person might. My hands grew cold. I shuddered. With this coldness, silence arrived, and I took my hands away from my eyes; they stung from the pressure of my palms having pressed against them. Blue lights danced against black, pulsating pathways of darkness. They evaporated and were replaced with a grey blur that came closer and closer. And as I focused, I saw their eyes staring into mine. To the left and right, eyes. The bulging eyes of the Ugly Children, their faces level with mine, their pupils fixed on me, their mouths open in stillborn Os. I stood to run; their eyes stood level with mine and they encircled me. The black hair of each child, strands of brambles, was entangled with the hair of the Ugly Child beside him. They called out to me in the persistent voices of the weak and desperate: *Guarzetto, vieni vieni con noi.* Come with us boy. *Zitto, zitto, zitto.* I ran, unable to escape. Their eyes surrounded me and no matter how fast I ran, they kept pace and enveloped me. A clap of thunder sounded and the rain began. I lost my footing in the mud and slid down the steep bank. I cried out, Go away, leave me alone.

Instantly, they were gone.

During the winter, I began to dream horrifically. I continued to suffer from terrifying episodes and I was preoccupied with thoughts of the Ugly Children. Every anecdote, every story, became a seed of fright that would take root without warning. Even a tale told by Gambetto one winter night grabbed hold of me.

The snow was falling when he held out his glass for a refill.

Do you know how stupid the people from Palugano are? he asked.

He looked me. No you couldn't know, you are too young. You live in a house of sensible people. You could never believe that people are any other way. How stupid they are, let alone how cruel. But I care only about the stupid because I can laugh at them. The cruel are something else. I don't want to talk about the cruel, that will be your problem. I'll be dead by the time they come to my door.

But the imbeciles, Gambetto said, *Dio cane*, that's my speciality. I am an expert on stupidity. On fools. An authority on asses and goats. A sage about men with heads of concrete and women with butterflies for brains.

So, he asked again, you know how stupid the people from Palugano are? It's far away, lucky for us. We don't have to drink the same water or marry their women, thank God. But you know how stupid those people there are? I'll tell you. You won't believe it.

These people, the whole town, the mayor, the butcher, the teacher, the nun, even the deaf-mute who should know better, are equally stupid. Do you know what they believe, these fools? They believe if you plant a pine needle, a pine tree will grow.

And so every fall, these morons go out into the woods and collect pine needles in their hats and aprons. And then, you know what they do?

They walk on the mountainside above the town and they plant these needles in the ground. You know why? They do it because they're afraid of a landslide and they think that if they can get a forest to grow above the town they won't be washed away. These fools, they cut down their trees and then try to start a new forest with pine needles. You see, one time a bird shat on the mountain, dropping a seed. A sapling grew, so they continue each year with this charade, thinking that it was a pine needle responsible for the tree and not a migrating bird.

But the best, the best, is that they walk around barefoot.

You know why? Why! Because one time someone cried, 'If we walk with our shoes we'll kill the poor baby saplings.' So now the whole town walks in the forest with no shoes. In the fall. After the freeze. When it snows and the ground is covered, then they put their shoes back on. And if it's a late snow, they suffer.

I listened to Gambetto, amazed, incredulous, that people could be so idiotic. Isaia sat away from the table half-smiling and laughing soundlessly. The others, Filomena, my Zia Albertina and Zio Erminio, urged Gambetto on. I wanted to hear no more about those stupid people and I looked to follow my grandfather's cue, for I was certain he would want no part of this silliness either. But he only continued to nod at Gambetto, puffing on his pipe. My mother sat with her needlework, amused and reserved.

Filomena hit the table and said to Gambetto, I heard, one time, something about their hunting abilities, what about that, Gambetto. Tell us. Tell us everything.

Good, I'm glad you brought that up, because it's another perfect example of the stupidity of the people from Palugano.

Zio Erminio leaned back in his chair, folded his thick arms and rested them on his chest. The women, except for my mother, leaned across the table. Gambetto waved on a refill of his glass. When it was full, he delicately grabbed it with the fingertips of his massive hands and centered it in front of him on the table.

One year, there was a plague of grasshoppers, of *grilli*.

These grasshoppers were everywhere. In the fountain, in the sugar bowls, in the confessional.

The mayor announced a campaign to eliminate the insects. He promised one lire for every grasshopper killed. And if the grasshopper still had wings, two lire. Well, these people went crazy, killing grasshoppers day and night, filling their sacks and their baskets.

So, anyway, listen, Gambetto said. There were two fools, who were no more stupid than the rest. And they had an idea to make a lot of money. Instead of using their shoes and switches, like the rest, they thought of something else.

The one said to the other that he knew how they could make a fortune with the grasshoppers.

How? said the other imbecile.

We'll take a gun. One of us can search them out and the other one can shoot.

And they caught a surprising number of grasshoppers in this way.

One afternoon, they were out in a field. Two grasshoppers landed on the chest of one of the men. He couldn't shout; he did not want to scare the grasshoppers away, so, instead he waved his arms, trying to the catch the eye of the other one. He pointed to the grasshoppers on his chest, mouthing the words, *Ammazz' i grilli.*

Kill the grasshoppers!

Right away, his partner aimed the gun, fired and killed the insects and the fool.

No, said my Zia Albertina. Is it true, Gambetto? Is it true?

True as the placement of the stars, Gambetto said. And then, you know the conclusion of the story, don't you?

No, Gambetto, finish, finish.

Well, he said drawing a breath, when the people went to collect their money for killing the grasshoppers, the mayor said there was no money in the treasury. The next day, it was learned he had run down to the plains and was never heard from again.

Gambetto looked at me and told me that whenever you see someone from Palugano, this is how you taunt him: as he walks toward you, point to your chest and whistle.

It was this story, one impoverished town's mockery of another town just as poor, that became confused with all the other new things I was learning, for that winter, cloistered at Tavolanuda, I also learned long division, my grandfather Isaia instructing me during the endless evenings. He warned: Keep your columns straight or you will lose the farm. He admonished: Multiply wrong and they will steal your sheep.

I had entered a new realm that brought more responsibility with little relief. How could I, one child, be held responsible for carelessly failing to carry over to the next column? I retreated further into myself, saying little. Every new thing I learned added to my anxiety; nothing gave comfort. In a pile of dead leaves, there could be buried, the *trombetto dei morti,* the death trumpet, covered in colors of black and grey, its edges draped like a shroud. Its character? Harmless. Its taste, satisfying. Likewise the *boletus lurido,* with its menacing name, was a delicacy. Isaia had shown me two strange-looking mushrooms. The *manine rosse* looks like a cauliflower, a great white trunk with red-tipped, truncated branches. Its name means "little pink hands," its pink tips reaching upward at the top of the body like the sunbaked hands of a thousand peasants with arms outstretched. The other one was its cousin, the *clavaria formosa,* which looked like a creature of the sea, its body the color and shape of coral. In this case, it was the *clavaria formosa,* which looked like a jewel, that was toxic; the *manine rosse,* ruddy supplicant, was safe. I had begged to be allowed to enter the apprenticeship, and once an initiate, I wanted to retreat.

No one noticed my silence and they could not hear the roaring inside of me. I told neither my mother nor my grandfather about the episodes of panic, which now occurred two or three times a week. Dyspnea, palpitation, paresthesia. These words are hollow and cannot convey the intensity of the attacks. Like the fluttering of the wings of bats inside the lungs, as a poet wrote.

I dreamed strange dreams.

In the midst of a snowstorm, in the middle of winter, I dreamed of hatted fairies in a circle. Hundreds of them, in their everyday garb, in their everyday colors: milk-white, marigold, lemon, acorn, peach, hushed violet. I looked on from above, seeing only the tops of the ladylike hats, wide brims that blocked my view. Then I walked underneath the brims, and I looked up from a great distance below. Distant as the moon, they were pleated silk fans touched by candlelight, luminescent against a black, starless sky. I leaned my head back. I was dizzy and nauseated. I stumbled. And then I woke up.

It was dark and there was no sound in the house. Beside me, Isaia slept. Convulsed, terrified, I began my ritual to calm myself. I said, I am Costante. I live at Tavolanuda with my grandmother and grandfather Isaia. My mother, Beatrice.

Next, in my mind, I travelled around the room.

The window. It looks to the valley. Under the window is the threshing floor and chicken yard. There is a cherry tree and a medlar. In this room, next to the window, is a chair. On the wall next to the chair is the wardrobe. Our clothes are folded there inside. Outside the door, across the hall my mother sleeps. On the wall outside her door hangs a picture of St. Christopher, gigantic St. Christopher, carrying the Christ Child on his shoulder across a river. My shoes are downstairs by the door. And now I am back in my bed again. Isaia sleeps and I am asleep as well.

But I was not. The wind picked up and the covers over my head could not block the sound. I stayed motionless, unable to sleep. Isaia stirred; he did not wake. I could no longer stay in bed. I slid my legs over the side of the bed and at last my toes touched the frigid pavement. I ran to the chair for my socks and shirt, then went downstairs to the hearth. In the dark, I sat in the chair next to the fireplace, which was my grandfather's chair. With a shawl pulled around me, knees drawn, I rocked myself back and forth, back and forth.

I followed the wind to Palugano, where the town of idiots walked barefoot in the snow, looking for pine needles. I sat on the fountain watching them, saying, You may put your shoes on. It is winter now and nothing will grow. But they did not listen and the deaf-mute spoke and said to everyone, The earth is starting to move! Look! And no one heard him or took note that he was speaking. The villagers walked around the piazza picking mushrooms from the snow, mostly the innocuous *prugnolo*. I saw a boy pick *the tignosa di primavera* and tried to warn that it would kill him. I pointed to my chest and waved my arms but he was transformed into the mayor and stood above me on the fountain and said to everyone who was now gathered around and wearing shoes because it was autumn: We have a blight of grasshoppers. I hereby order you to kill every grasshopper and bring them to me so that I will have enough to eat. If you leave just one alive, I will order you all to eat poisonous mushrooms. The mayor turned into the boy again and he jumped off the fountain into a fairy ring and started swinging his flail in every direction, lashing out at the long-legged creatures and cutting them to the ground. I followed behind and saw what he did. Gambetto was sitting under the lone chestnut, and I told him about the boy, begged him to make the boy stop, but he said: I discourse only about the stupid; the cruel I leave to you. And he called for more wine. I ran up to the boy to divert him, to tell him the secret of the gossiping fairies, but he raised his flail and continued to swing at the mushrooms in the field, *orecchione, manine rosse, spugnole gialle,* mushrooms of every kind were there on the ground, and the boy's flail turned into a gun and he started blowing apart the mushrooms until the grasshoppers underneath were exposed. He kept shooting and saying, *Ammazz' i grilli, grilli matti.* Kill the grasshoppers, crazy grasshoppers. *Grilli matti, grilli pazzi.* Boom. Boom. Boom. And the grasshoppers cried louder and louder, filling the valley with a plea, a high-pitched wail, a desperate choked insect voice that shrieked, *Qui, qui, qui, ni cià guarzetto, aiutami, aiutami, zitto, zitto, zitto, aiutami, ni cià, guarzetto, 'zitto, e te stad zitto.* Come here, they said, come here, here, boy, help me, help me, quiet, shhh, shhh, help me, here, boy, boy, and you remain here silent.

The boy blasted the insects with his gun and as he shot, the creatures were transformed into the Ugly Children and all around, I saw their wide-open eyes, stretched open in terror, their hair wild from flight, from fright, and they followed me and called for help, while their siblings lay slain in the field, pine needles scattered about, and the boy with the gun blasted, and I froze with trepidation, terrorized by the boy who was laying waste to my tormenters.

When war came fourteen years later, and then again in my middle years, Isaia was not there to guide me. Many men were removed far away, many places were forsaken. And there was no voice, like far-off thunder saying, *Indemma.* Let's go.

31

Waiting for Giotto

At dusk, he crosses the threshing floor. The soles of his wooden shoes hit against the stones. The stones fit closely, embedded into the ground, squared blocks pressed tightly, one against the other such that no weed can grow between them. The threshing floor is Apennine sandstone, slate-grey, and not easily splintered.

❧

When he exhales, his breath is visible in the faltering light. Below, to his left, in the valley, a bell pounds five times, a hollow knocking toll. He pauses and looks. In Ardonlà, minute lights begin to flicker; the river has already disappeared in the dark. The mountain peak and ridges are looming hunchbacked beasts.

He whistles, a sharp, cranium-piercing whistle, and Diana the goat trots up beside him and follows. He is a tall, gangly man, all limbs and neck. He approaches the stable, leans a shoulder into the door, loosening it, lowering his head as he passes underneath the lintel.

Inside, he lights one candle and sets it up high on a shelf, out of the way, so that it will not be accidentally toppled. A tunic falls to just above his knees; it is a plush material, a purple so deep it is almost black.

Diana the goat settles into the corner and is sleeping like a patient dog.

He takes a panel from the corner, unwinds the piece of sackcloth that covers it. He hangs the cloth on a wooden peg. The panel of chestnut has been planed and smoothed, then coated with lime, which dried, and then was rubbed and smoothed some more. He lays the wooden panel on freshly scattered straw and drops to his haunches, his long legs bent and splayed, the heavy cloth of the tunic draping over his knees.

With jagged fingernails, he scratches his scalp and his arm. Patches of skin have turned white, then red, and he must try not to touch them. The skin throbs and pulls apart from itself, and when he can no longer tolerate it, his nails nick hatch marks into the skin, and the sting relieves his incessant discomfort.

Bartolomeo de Bartolai stares down at what he has drawn: three faces, one floating above the other. Three bodiless beings. Each face is round, with wide, almond-shaped eyes that stare out, impassive and severe, orbs that nearly fill the socket. Each pupil is obsidian, a perfectly round stone. Above the eyes, the thick brows merge together and form a painted gash. He gives each face a tiny, set mouth. In the place of a body, there is an arc, a boat whose prow and stern fan upward into wings. He has copied these figures from angels chiseled in stone above the door of his farmhouse, the work of his grandfather's father. The men of the mountains all know how to work with stone, they can chisel celestial beings from it. His nails are dirty. His fingers are scraped and cut, stiff from the cold. He comes into this stable at night, while the others quietly drink their aqua vita in front of the hearth, dulling their hunger, numbing their sores.

By day he tends the sheep, in the evening he comes to the stable. It is the second night of November in 1560.

The winter is long. Bartolomeo de Bartolai sits drawing on a flat piece of rock, over and over. He draws with clay dug from a ravine and ash taken from the hearth. He draws with charred twigs of chestnut and hawthorn, with charred walnut shells. He makes drawings on flat stones and rough wood. Drawings of what? The usual things. The things that he knows. Sheep. Goats. Everyday things.

Bartolomeo de Bartolai lives in a remote narrow valley, far away from a city, but knows the story of Giotto, the greatest artist in the history of the world, word of Giotto has made its way even this far. He knows how Giotto's father was a simple fellow who gave his son sheep to tend. How the boy was forever drawing on stones, on the ground, in sand, on anything, and how, one day, he was discovered, by the great painter Cimabue, who saw the boy drawing a sheep on a flat, polished stone. How Cimabue asked the father for permission to take the boy Giotto to Florence, and the father lovingly granted permission. Bartolomeo de Bartolai knows this story, the holy men themselves disseminated it, and he has heard how Giotto, single-handedly, restored good design and drawing to Christendom after it was corrupted by the infidels.

So many others have left to find a way in the world. Others younger than he, who were babies when he was already tending sheep.

He watched them leave with canvas sacks upon their backs, depart and not look behind. From his spot near the river, he was stunned and astonished: They were not waiting. How did they conceive such a thing?

He wanted to say, Stop! You are not ready to go yet! You are too young to set off in the world. This is not how you are supposed to do it. You are supposed to do it like this: sit here by a river, drawing, like me, drawing, drawing, shapes and lines and figures, making them look like they are moving in three dimensions. It is very difficult. You will not necessarily understand the shapes you are making, but you must keep making them and a picture will emerge. Slowly, slowly, until one day, they will dance upon the rock. This is how it must be done. You must serve an apprenticeship, here.

But they did not. They were bold. They told the priest, You have nothing more to teach me. They said to their parents, I break with you.

He watched them leaving, climbing the hill, through the gate of the walled town, up the side of the mountain toward Faidello, up higher toward the house of Abramo, toward the Long Forest and over the hill toward Cutigliano, on to Pistoia. Pistoia, where they have invented a tool, a handheld weapon that exhales explosion. A pistol. These people who were younger than him headed past Pistoia, past Prato, where abandoned babies are left at the hospice of the Misericordia. They went down the slopes of the foothills, where grapes and acacia grow, onto the plain, into the river bed of the Arno, into the city, Fiorenza.

He envied them, but crossed himself and prayed, because *invidia* is a sin. The envious sinners in purgatory, between the Wrathful and Proud. He saw the others leaving, bounding away, and thought, Do they not risk worse sins?

No, he wanted to shout. Wait. Wait right here with me. Wait your turn. Do not risk abandonment. Come sit beside me; I have been practicing, practicing for years. Come wait with me.

He opened his mouth to shout, he could see them up the hill, but his throat was dry and no sound came out.

⚜

Before he can make his way down from the mountains, he must learn the principles; this is his understanding. And so he has prepared and prepared and prepared. Before you even begin to contemplate the journey, you must understand certain things. The principle of perspective. Vanishing point.

Bartolomeo de Bartolai sits making figures on a panel of wood, over and over, waiting for Giotto.

⚜

He scavenges and hoards, and whenever he finds a broken plate, a cracked vase, a shattered bottle from the midwife, he gathers the pieces in a canvas sack that hangs from his waist. This sack is called a *scarsella*, an alms purse. Since no one in these mountains possesses coins to fling to beggars, a *scarsella* is any type of gathering sack, whether for mushrooms or for chestnuts.

Whenever he goes to town, to Ardonlà, on market days, he wears the *scarsella* and walks behind the shops on either side of the street to see what has been discarded. Once he found an apothecary jar, broken and without its lid, decorated with blue and yellow scrolls. He gathered the pieces of this ointment jar, wrapped the fragments in a rag, then put the bundle under his cloak. He looked to see what was behind the shop of the blacksmith. Nothing. And behind the tinker. Nothing. Beside the church, he found a broken chalice, made of wine-red glass, which the priest had unblessed and thrown into a heap. Behind the tavern, he found a broken string of beads, pieces of flat blue glass, and he took these as well.

For this scrounging, his mother cuffs the back of his head. At least leave intact our dignity, so that we are not seen picking up broken things from people who have as little as we do. They will call us mendicants and hoarders. But Bartolomeo de Bartolai cannot stop himself from squatting down to pick up a shard if it glints.

He saves the collected fragments in a chest inside the stable.

⚜

Halfway down the valley, the windows of the villa are filled with panes of glass. When the Signore married a lady from Ferrara, he put in glass that came all the way from Venezia. In Venezia, he has heard, there are hordes of men and women and children, arrived from the mountains, who work in shops making glass. How dazzling it would be to live there. Bartolomeo de Bartolai imagines a city of glass, color reflecting everywhere. He imagines heaps of glass everywhere, glistening like the mounds of jewels inside a sultan's tomb. Whenever a glassmaker makes an error, or inadvertently drops a bottle, he tosses the broken pieces into a heap. He has heard of a young person who travelled to Venezia and is etching spectacular mountains on the insides of vases. In Venezia, the brilliance would only blind him and cause him to wince. Here, instead, he can keep his eyes open, scanning the ground for the rare discarded colored piece.

How were those others able to leave so soon? Not sit up here and wait? He saw their proud chins jutted forward. He saw how they waved to him as they passed by. He believes they saw him as a simple person, sitting there with his sheep. He wanted to remind them that Giotto was a shepherd, but they would not have cared. They would have said, You are left behind by time. They do not even recall Cimabue, he is irrelevant to them, and their gazes are fixed beyond the mountain pass.

He sits and waits for a master, someone to tap his shoulder, to lift him up, usher him by the elbow. Invite him into apprenticeship. Perhaps Giotto himself, stern in profile, will see the drawings, his fine collection of shards, and will say, Yes. Then lead him away, down out of the mountains.

Once, he went to see a great man as the entourage passed on the road above, he had heard he was a great painter. Everyone clapped and sang as the man approached, reached out their hands to him. Young men carried the great man on their backs, on a chair fastened to poles. They sank down in the mud to their knees. From the side of the road, Bartolomeo de Bartolai stretched out his arm, and the great man mimicked the way his hand trembled.

He looks up into the face of each stranger passing through, wondering if he is the Master. Each season, the Giotto he envisions has a different face.

He sits and he waits for Giotto; he knows better than to wait for Cimabue. Too much time has passed. He lives below a narrow dirt road, a mule path no more than three men wide, the only road that passes through the mountains and links one city to another. He lives in a cluster of ten houses that is too small to be called a hamlet. One house touches the other, and they are all made of the same grey stone as the cliff. The houses sit on a ledge supported by a single granite column. It is called *La Gruccia,* the *crutch,* because from a distance it looks as if it were perched on a walking stick.

Giotto might travel some day along the mule path above. He might stop because he needed to sleep. Or because he needed to eat. Because his horse was tired. Giotto would somehow know that Bartolomeo de Bartolai was sitting by the edge of the river drawing figures of sheep on stone, just as Giotto himself had done, and surely, he would appreciate this diligence.

Did the ones who have gone down receive a call? Because no one goes down without an invitation. How did it enter their minds that they were worthy enough to knock on the door of the privileged? A shepherd does not go through the gates of a rich man's house, not even to a door around back, unless he knows that there is someone who will answer. He knows he would be apprehended, arrested, beaten, put outside the gate to starve. He would be mistaken for a vagrant. Who are they, the ones who went down? These privileged ones who have taken it upon themselves to go down to a master's shop?

He knows that the ones who have left would mock him: That old man, what do you want with that old man? He has nothing to teach you. No one has anything to teach you that you cannot learn by yourself. You are wasting time; your life is passing. Count the days already gone. In winter you could die suddenly of pneumonia; in summer, contagion travels up from the plain. What do you wait for? An invitation on parchment? With gilt edges, rolled tightly into a scroll? Bah, they would say, these young people with sacks hoisted over their shoulders, their chins in the air. Bah. There is no messenger that brings correspondence intended for these parts; the only messages are those that travel through, being carried from one city on the plains to another. This Giotto you wait for is archaic. His students have moved beyond him. They have already stood on his shoulders and seen things he could not dream of. You are too solicitous, too timid. You defer, when you should demand.

But I am only a simple shepherd.

The bell down in the village bongs seven times, a slow weighted rumble. Outside the shed, the sky is black.

He sits on straw in the stable at night and remembers a fresco at a church, the pilgrims' destination, the monastery of San Pellegrino, built on a pinnacle where three valleys come together. The monks say this fresco was done by Giotto.

He carried away the fresco, holds the picture inside his head: San Gioacchino is asleep on the ground in the mountain, chased from the temple into the mountains because he has fathered no children. He wears a rose-colored robe. He is sitting, head on arm, which is resting on his knee. While he is asleep, an angel announces that his barren wife is with child, and that the child will become the mother of God. A shepherd leans on a crutch. One sheep stands on a granite scarp. Another one sleeps. A black goat looks away, while a ram sits wide awake. They are all fat, healthy creatures. The halo of the sleeping saint is golden. A gorse plant nearby is flecked with yellow.

On a piece of stone, Bartolomeo de Bartolai imitates the way the rib cage of the shepherd's dog is visible through its skin, the way the goat's hoof splays as it steps down the side of a cliff.

When Bartolomeo de Bartolai looks around, he sees that all the young people have gone down out of the mountains. One, whom he called friend, Martín de Martinelli, patted him on the head, and then was gone like the rest. He last heard that Martín was in Fiorenza preparing walls for frescoes.

When he left, Martín de Martinelli did not look back or sideways; he had always been preparing to leave. Those who move away carry off what they wish and remake in their minds those who have stayed, while the ones who remain behind are left to wonder what has become of those who depart. Some who stay in the mountains close their hearts tight to forget the ones who have left; some turn the departed into heroes, making them more than they are. And if those who have ventured out should return, the ones who have remained lose voice in their presence because the returning emigrants claim the expertise of the world.

As a child, Bartolomeo de Bartolai followed after this friend, imitating him. He was intrigued, intimidated. It was excessive adoration. His heart is hardened, and yet he still hopes for a single message. Like a puppy dog. Then he wishes to kick himself for this suppliance, but does not. He turns back into himself and makes marks on stones.

Why was he so dazzled by Martín de Martinelli, a person who treated others like servants? Finally he understands what he had refused to see for so long: Martín de Martinelli is the earth and everyone else is a planet circling.

Martín de Martinelli would occasionally glance over his shoulder as he sat bent over a panel of wood, commenting upon his progress. Bartolomeo de Bartolai wants to know if noteworthiness is like this? Others watching to see if you might be recognized, if you are the one who will go to work in the shop of a master. They watch, afraid of approaching too close lest you remain forever hunched over, eccentric and obscure. It was an infatuation, he decides, a kind of being in love with Martín de Martinelli, with a person incapable of listening. How do you comprehend the world if you see only yourself, over and over and over? Do you see yourself finally as a spectre? As spectre, you then consume the air around you like a flame. And while some pull up cushions to sit at your feet, you fail to notice that others have wandered off, neglected and stung. One person in town called Martín de Martinelli a trinket maker of worthless things, spoiled, and Bartolomeo de Bartolai said, No, there is genius, wait. I was young, he thinks now. Spellbound. But the truth is, I wanted his way of being for myself, his ease and his boldness. Now I see that these thoughts were a form of Envy, and that this elaborate infatuation was Covetousness, and that I coveted his signature.

He blames others for his timidity:

His great-grandmother who was once a lioness and now does not know her own daughter.

His grandmother who must tend to her and grips his wrist when he passes by.

His mother who drinks a bitter liquid made from distilled walnuts, each time the great-grandmother wails.

His father who leaves the house and wanders into the woods to escape. Bartolomeo de Bartolai stays in the corner waiting to see if his mother will call out for him; when he leaves, his father pats him on the head, and calls him his favorite child, though he knows his favorite child is the one who has stayed, the one who is huddled in the kitchen with a wrist being gripped.

He stays. He waits. He holds his great-grandmother's hand in the dim light while she moans. His grandmother begs him to tell her what is beyond the threshold and he describes the garb of the pilgrims. The painted cart of the book merchant and the books laden onto the back of a mule. Bartolomeo de Bartolai puts a cool cloth on his mother's forehead after she has fallen asleep. He unbolts the door for his father when he comes back home. They all grow old.

It is a new era, the ones who left have said. The old order is gone. Be bold, be deferential no more.

※

There is calm as his hand moves across a flat, polished stone. He draws, draws, draws, and on his way back from the fields into the house he tosses the stone into a pile in a corner of the threshing floor. The literate call the threshing floor an *aia*. Aye-a. Like a scream. From all the being beaten down. The peasants like him call it an *ara*, which also means *altar*.

※

Before they go off, when the journey is still before them, do they feel the twinge of misgiving? In the months before they leave, the impending journey has already changed them. Every encounter becomes a question: Will this be the final encounter? So that in the future you will say, The last time I saw Martín, he was at the fountain in town. But if you should see him once more, this is how he is remembered: The last time I saw Martín, he was in the tavern, playing *tresette* and winning. Once he announced his desire to leave, he could never be Martín in the same way again; he became Martín-who-will-leave-in-September. Once he revealed his intention to leave, he ceased to be part of the daily flow of mundane activity, bodies leaning into plows, planting, training vines against a trellis, harvesting, threshing, butchering a hog, coming into a stone house silently from the snow. He could not be part of the winter's circle around the hearth, or, when the sun emerged in the spring, he was no longer one who replaced slate tiles upon a roof or gathered early berries. At the moment he said he was leaving, Martín de Martinelli placed himself outside all this. It was irreversible. Even if he had changed his mind at the last instant, others would have thought, This year he stayed, but next year? He was no longer part of day-to-day movement, taking tools to the blacksmith or standing against the side of the mountain at the mill as grain was being ground, talking loudly above the roar of the cascade. When the wax of candles dripped onto the stone floor of the church at midnight on Christmas, he was not part of the chanting.

But wasn't it always so, the leaving? Is not the Holy Book that is read on Sunday the story of departure, one after another after another? Were not these mountains populated by nomads with tents and sheep? The Etrurian people coming up from the plains, some of whom buried the bones of their dead, some of whom buried their ashes in urns. They were followed by Christians who prayed in caves and, then, by Roman soldiers deserting, who were followed by the red-haired, blue-eyed ones with their bagpipes made of sheep gut who built stone huts here, warriors from the north with massive beards and long, consonant-filled words. Then the descendants of Esther fleeing the walled cities on the plains, accused of killing infants. They all fled into the mountains, staggering up here, burying their dead along the way. Trying to outrun war and pestilence. For centuries and centuries, they came up into the mountains. Bartolomeo de Bartolai is all of them. Who can say where he began, and who was the one who begat the person who begat him, who begat that person, all the way back to the beginning? Back to the gods of the northmen. Back to Job.

A man who came back from the Orient with Marco Polo was beaten in Venezia; they beat him on the stone floor under an alcove in the calle dell'Arco. And this man made his way southward to Ravenna, from which he was driven to other cities, Forlì, Ímola, Bologna, skirting the edge of the mountains, persecuted the entire way, until he was driven into a blind alley in Modena by thugs, nearly set afire, and he fled upward, up, up, up, into the mountains. He ran to the highest point, until he could go no farther without descending. He begged for mercy at the feet of the oldest woman of the village who stared down at this man with pitch-black hair. He did not want to go back down onto the plains; he begged her in his native tongue, and because he had a wide smile like her last-born son who had fallen off the mountain, she said to him, You may stay and be safe. As she spoke, the others dropped their clubs; one man gave him a massive shepherd's coat, a coat made of skins. He showed the others how to weave reeds into mats of intricate patterns. He built a strange, stringed instrument. He married, and his wife bore twelve children, six of whom survived. Scattered stone houses hold altars dedicated to a forgotten god whose name means immeasurable light.

The ancestors, yes, were nomads and people in flight, but, once here, they stayed put and lived their lives according to the rhythm of the bell, resounding morning, noon and night; and the seasons, summer, autumn, winter, spring; and all the rituals and holy days that are repeated in order, in an endless variation. His ancestors of long, long ago were people in motion, but they were followed by people, he believes, who should remain in this same place, immovable and bound to this soil.

He crosses the *ara* in the fading light of autumn. He sits on straw in a corner of the stable. He picks up a stone and draws. When he is exhausted, he returns to the house and lays his head on a mattress filled with wood shavings and scented with thyme to keep away insects. He dreams of a tap on the shoulder. He dreams about forms, a dog's paw, the curve of an angel's chin. A scaffold. He sees his hand move across a piece of stone, leaving identifiable marks, a sparrow, a lamb that looks as if it could bleat for its mother. He dreams of drawing pictures whole.

At the church of San Pellegrino, he once saw ten angels in a storm-blue sky, and they were all lamenting what occurred below. One threw its head backward, open arms and palms outstretched downward as if pushing away the air. One scratched and tore the skin of its cheeks with its fingernails; another pulled golden strands of hair outward from its scalp. One held a pale yellow cloth up close to its open eyes, as if wanting to conceal the view. The bodies of these angels tapered, then disappeared like flames.

The fresco in the pilgrims' church was a copy, painted by some-one who had imitated a fresco down lower in the mountains, which was in turn an imitation of one in the foothills, which was a copy of one from down lower still, an imitation of a fresco in a town on the river, which was a modified version of a fresco farther downriver, a fresco which was an imitation of one in the city. The first one to copy it was called a follower of Giotto, and even after all these copies, the fresco in the mountains at the pilgrims' church site bears the great man's name.

❧

He dreams of drawing pictures whole, but whenever he begins, he falters.

Martín de Martinelli said, Once silenced, we have been un-silenced.

But Bartolomeo de Bartolai sits there knowing that he still stut-ters, tentative, trepid, trembling.

Tiresome, he knows, and reminds himself he possesses worldly goods: he has a pallet with blankets. He has spiritual wealth. He has all of his fingers and teeth.

When he opens his mouth to say he is timid and weak, to say he cannot speak, a voice behind him says, What, then, is the sound com-ing from your mouth?

❧

Do you remember how in our youth we rebelled? Martín de Martinelli had said before he left. Do you not recall?

Bartolomeo de Bartolai had replied, *Yes.* But all he remembered were words half-formed in his mouth.

Do you remember how we added our names to the list of demands signed by Iacomo de Petro, Lorenzo de Contro, Rolandino de Berton?

Yes, he said. But in truth he could not write his name.

Boldly, they took down the banner of the duke, and hoisted up another at night in the dark. They fled deep into the woods and sang songs around a fire, and when the sun rose in the morning, the people in the village of Ardonlà woke to find the sky-blue herald of the dissidents suspended from an arch.

Certain reproaches still clang in his ears: The hierarchy has crumbled; we are no longer serfs.

When, on the mule path above, a handbell is rung six times but not at the sixth hour, it means travellers are passing through and are looking for food to purchase. Itinerant merchants, soldiers. Or pilgrims en route to holy places:

San Pellegrino dell'Alpe, they chant,
scendete un po' più giù
abbiam rotto le scarpe
non ne possiamo più.

The penitent traveller says this aloud walking toward the relics of San Pellegrino, the hermit who lived in a hollowed-out beech tree.

San Pellegrino, they mumble aloud,
come down a bit lower,

we have broken our shoes

and cannot go any farther.

Once, eleven years ago, when he heard the bell ringing, Bartolomeo de Bartolai carried up a wooden pail filled with milk; he had no cheese to sell. He climbed the footpath up the side of the mountain, the branches of the hedges brushing his arm, the saw-toothed canes of blackberries pricking through his leggings, the sun beating down on his back.

He arrived at the road out of breath. It was July and pilgrims were travelling south and west toward the mountain pass on their way to the monastery of San Pellegrino. A pilgrim gestured to him. Bartolomeo de Bartolai saw that despite her simple garb of hazel-colored wool, despite her display of poverty, she was privileged; she wore a thick gold ring on a golden chain around her neck. Her alms purse was bulging. Bartolomeo de Bartolai stood in front of her, holding his pail, looking at the ground, waiting to be spoken to.

Mid-conversation, she spoke to another pilgrim. She was not going to the pilgrimage site of San Pellegrino, like the rest, she said, but rather to the south and east, toward the city of Fiorenza. Then she began speaking of the master Giotto:

Giotto apprenticed with Cimabue for ten years.

Bartolomeo de Bartolai stared at the ground, listening.

The Pope called him to Rome for the Jubilee in 1300, and Giotto worked on the basilica of San Giovanni in Laterno.

Bartolomeo de Bartolai offered her the pail of milk. She batted him away and called her lady-in-waiting.

In that city, he made a mosaic called La Navicella in the portico of St. Peter's, a mosaic of Christ walking on water.

He listened, open-mouthed. The lady-in-waiting approached and grabbed the pail from him.

In Padova, he painted the Scrovegni chapel, where I myself have prayed, and there is an imitation of it at the pilgrims' church in these savage mountains.

The lady-in-waiting handed the pail to a manservant.

In Assisi, he painted San Francesco's life.

The manservant poured the milk into a large metal flask. The servants watched their lady speak.

He painted the great poet Dante from life.

The manservant thrust the pail back to him.

As she turned to go, Bartolomeo de Bartolai bowed his head and asked the lady, *And, please tell me, on these journeys, what kind of materials does the artist Giotto pack into sacks and transport?*

The pilgrim backed away from him, wrapping her cloak around her, covering her mouth and her nose, and said, *What do you think I am, a book?*

He had seen what a book looked like, he had seen people with their noses looking down into books. So when she said to him, What do you think I am, a book? he was stung, humiliated. He did not know how to understand her insult. He knew that she was not a book; a book is an inanimate object. A book is made of paper, which is made from trees, and the trees come from forests in the mountains because all of the great forests of the plains have been leveled. No, she was not a book, she was a woman with raven hair visible at the edge of her hood.

But he remembers to this day what the humbly clad pilgrim said, what he overheard: Giotto painted Dante from life. Bartolomeo de Bartolai does not understand this expression. How else would he have painted him? From death? No, because a painting or mosaic comes from an idea, and an idea is alive. Something you hear or see or smell or touch or taste puts a picture into your head, and this causes you to put down a mark. She was trying to impress them with her knowledge of the world down there, of how far she had travelled, then became offended because she was asked a question she could not answer: What materials does Giotto use? Of course Giotto painted Dante from life; he painted everything from life, a goat with splayed hooves, a shepherd with a tattered hem.

Of course, Bartolomeo de Bartolai knows what a book is. He has seen them at the villa of the Signore. He was shown a page once, during the month of August, when he and his father were summoned to the villa. They were asked to move a wardrobe from one room to another. They hoisted it with great difficulty and carried it on their backs across the hall into another room. The Signore was not sure where he wanted it placed, so he went upstairs to ask his wife, the lady from Ferrara for whom he had put in glass windows. They set down the wardrobe, and while the Signore was gone, Bartolomeo de Bartolai gazed around the room at the polished marble floor with its swirling of onyx and pavonazzo purple and umber.

In the corner, Bartolomeo de Bartolai saw a strange piece of furniture. As tall as his waist, it stood on a single leg, like a crane, a *gru*. There was a tray at the top made of two pieces of wood that fit together and lay like a bird's open wings. A book rested on top. The Signore's voice and footsteps were still upstairs, and Bartolomeo de Bartolai peered down into the open book, careful not to breathe on it.

One page was a wall of marks. One page was a drawing. The

drawing was this: two circles side by side. Inside the circle on the right was a form with a rounded back, the profile of a monster with a single eye of ultramarine. Inside the other circle was a pair of curved claws that reached up toward the monster.

The Signore swept in and saw him looking. His father raised a hand to cuff him, but the Signore stopped him and said to Bartolomeo de Bartolai, Do you like my book? I bought it in Venezia for three *scudi*. You can buy any book you want in Venezia; it is where most of them are published. In that city, a man is free to think his own thoughts and ideas circulate freely. The thoughts of the reformers are openly discussed. Some doubt the existence of hell, some deny the Trinity.

He pointed to the book and placed an index finger on certain marks, pronouncing the words *Orbis Descriptio*.

This is a map of the world. He pointed to the circle on the right. This is the Old World, and this blue oval is the Mediterranean. We are the Old World.

Then, he pointed to the circle on the left. This is the New World. The Arctic, the territory of Florida, the Terra Incognita of the interior, which all belongs to Spain. Below, America of the South.

Bartolomeo de Bartolai would like him to point out other places, for example, where is Fiorenza? He would like to see where Giotto has travelled. But instead, the Signore says: I have decided after all to put the piece of furniture back into the room where it was originally. On the way out, the Signore tells them that behind the stables there is an old pine board from a table top which they are welcome to take.

At twilight, that evening, he went back down to the villa. He walked through the villa's forest-garden, where the Signore planted pine trees so they formed the letters *V* and *L*, the initials of the Signora. In a corner of this walled forest-garden was a heap of discarded objects, and there Bartolomeo de Bartolai found the pine board.

For months the board has lain untouched in the corner of the stable; he is afraid to make a mark on it, does not want to spoil it.

⁂

Each night, he walks out to the stable, seeking a respite from the house where his great-grandmother sits on a mat in the corner and moans and rocks, her eyes wide and staring at nothing. His grand-mother feeds her chestnut gruel with a wooden spoon. The great-grandmother spits the food back out. The grandmother clears her mother's lips with the edge of the spoon. His grandmother grabs the wrist of whoever is nearest, whoever is passing by, whoever is most alive. In springtime, his mother sings of the harvest, *The day laid on the threshing floor is flayed.* She sings love songs all day long. His father bends his head under the granite lintel as he passes through the door-way; his shoulders brush the frame, though he is not a large man, and he slams the door shut. His grandmother grabs him by the wrist and his mother sings. In the day, he takes his cloth hat from the bench and follows his father out the door. He goes off into the field, and watches after the five thin sheep and the three emaciated goats.

In order to pay for grazing rights for a season, when he was a boy, his mother cut his hair. She pulled it tight, away from his head, cut it close to the scalp. Then she sold it to a pillow merchant passing through. After she cut his hair, he would run down the path into the field, where everything was blurred from tears, and he pointed out the grass to the beasts, showing them which blades to eat.

⁂

As he stands up to go out to the stable, he carries a lantern be-cause darkness comes early. They begrudge him oil for the lamp. His mother says, Where do you think more oil will come from? You think it will seep out of a crack in a stone? His father says, When a spark turns into a ball of fire what will we do then? This is the discussion every night, every night at dusk, when his uncle and great-uncle, his grandfather's brother, get ready to tell the stories they have told again and again, the same ones, how a grave robber dug up the bones of San Sisto in Rome and tried to sell them to priests all the way up into the mountains, but no one believed him, and, desperate because he was high up in the mountains in winter and without any money, he sold them to a wealthy old woman, who bought the bones with one gold *genovino* and a sword and a bundle of candles, and as soon as he handed the relics to the old woman, he was turned into a pillar of stone, and she had a chapel built right there. He does not want to hear any more of these stories, he has heard them every night of his life: how the poor young man found a key that let him into the princess's heart, how the charcoalmaker's son solved three riddles. He begs them for oil for the lamp. His mother accuses him: *spende fina i capei;* he would spend even the hair on his head. At the villa of the Signore, the lan-terns burn all night long, yet they accuse him of being profligate for trying to extend the day.

His father hollers, And if you start an inferno? His mother hollers, If we run out of light? Then his grandmother grabs his wrist and holds it up to them and says, You cut his hair, you sold it, now give the child some light.

If he could, he would write the master Giotto a letter. Tell him that he is ready to come down and work in his shop, to mix plaster, to clean paintbrushes. If only to rake, with a wooden pitchfork, the stall where his horse sleeps at night.

※

In the stable, he cleans a spot on the dirt and lays the panel on the ground.

We are isolated, but we hear things. We are remote, but we see things.

He hears rumblings of what goes on below; the sounds echo up three valleys, the Valley of the Scoltenna, the Valley of the Dragon, the Valley of Light, and by the time the sound makes its way up into the mountains, after having bounced off mountain walls, it is only a faint echo. The sounds arrive belatedly, sometimes centuries later. He has heard the priest speak the word, FRACTUM. This is the way the sound comes up, in pieces. After something has already happened to fracture the whole into pieces.

He spills out the pieces of terra-cotta and broken glass and sifts through what he possesses.

※

What do you think I am, a book? He hears the words again and again. I have never left these mountains, but I know something of other places because people travelling through bring word, the itinerant monk, the copper seller, the merchant who buys flock and hair. They carry up messages from down below, and this is how it is possible to know something of other places. I have seen certain things with my own eyes, like the frescoes at the pilgrims' church, the saint sleeping in the mountains, ten angels wailing in the sky.

55

In his head, he continues to fight with Martín de Martinelli, ten years gone, thinks of how Martín de Martinelli said to him: Wake up! Raise up your eyes!

And how he replied, I have been taught to keep my head bowed and not to swagger, to not be a braggart and spendthrift like the prosperous shepherd who sees a little of the world, sells his fat sheep down on the plains, and comes back with coins in his pockets, blaspheming and knocking over tables in the tavern. I have been taught to be simple, honest, laborious. Labor is honor. All I have ever seen are heads bent over and down; look at the way everyone's shoulders are curved.

Look up, said Martín de Martinelli.

And Bartolomeo de Bartolai answered, You look up and you see misery. You see how the lords overrun one another's territory, spreading disaster, spreading strife. You see how brigands steal anything that glistens. How soldiers bring contagion and take away flour. You see starving mothers who leave infants to die on the mountainside so that the ones at home survive.

And Martín de Martinelli replied, The days of a peasant's false humility are over. Do you not see that a new day is coming which will do away with antiquated ways? Do you not see that there will be new systems to classify, new instruments to understand the world?

Bartolomeo de Bartolai asked him, Does it bring comfort to think that there will be instruments to measure cold and heat, that will measure the strength of wind and the weight of air? Will they not take away the hours of the day, the days in their merciful order? The seasons that make this life, with its empty stomach and lesions, bearable? Will it not take away the calendar that begins with the feast day of the Blessed Virgin and ends with the feast day of San Silvestro? Would you have me break this whole?

Martín de Martinelli said, I would not have you break anything. I am not here to cause you to do anything. I can only say what I am going to do: I am leaving. I am not going to remain up here, my stifled voice vibrating against the vocal cords. Do you know how it is when you have a great sadness, a great anger, and try to make no sound? Do you know how it is when you hold it inside your throat? Of course you know, because you are a mountain dweller, made of stone, and you think you can outlast the pain without opening your mouth.

Bartolomeo de Bartolai answered, I notice no such pain.

Martín de Martinelli said, If a dog catches his paw in a trap, and the paw is cut, it yelps and howls, and then, if the dog survives, and the wound heals, he becomes accustomed to the pain and merely winces each time he puts his weight upon the paw.

⚘

He must turn away from the admonishments; he must turn away and try to recall something else. Something beautiful. A mosaic. On the other side of the river above Ardonlà are the ruins of a fortress that sits on a steep bluff. Below it is a cave. The entryway is hidden among bushes and rocks along the riverbed. The passageway opens into caverns where Christians hid when they fled into the mountains. They were followers of Sant'Apollinaris of Ravenna. They built an altar in a cave, and, on the vault, they made a mosaic like the ones they had left behind. When it became safe, they built their altars above ground, and the ones below were forgotten. The forest above was cleared and a landslide buried the cave's entrance.

He saw the mosaics only once. He was a child. He was taken
there by his great-grandmother who is now being fed like a baby. She
was not afraid of wolves or bears, and she took his hand and led him
there. He was not afraid because she was not afraid. She was bent
over as she walked beside him, leaning on her wooden walking stick,
which was shaped like the letter *T.* She told him she was going to
show him where a saint was buried, told him that no one else remembered, that they were too afraid to look. As she walked, she became transformed and stood up straight; she threw away her walking
stick. She moved like a goat from one rock to another and she was not
afraid of slipping on a wet stone. All the lines were erased from her
face; her blue eyes were lights; she balanced on one rock, and then
another, along the bank of the river.

He is trying to see the mosaic again. There was a strange source
of light. There were foreign plants and creatures. A palm tree with
leaves that grew out from the center like the legs of a spider. A turtle
climbing out of the water onto a bank. There were two cranes drinking from a pedestal fountain.

At night, he crosses the *ara,* and sits on the straw with a sackcloth blanket covering his legs. The lantern hangs on a wooden peg.
On the floor, there is a jar containing mastic, which he has made from
the resin of pine. Before him on a rag, he has spread out the fragments
of broken glass and painted terra-cotta. Each night, he lays out a row,
edging one piece against another.

He thinks, We hear things up in the mountains. We are isolated, but we hear things, just as we heard of Giotto. Just as we have heard that in France on the other side of the river called the Var, men slaughter each other. One man slashes the gullet of the other, like a pig is killed before dressing, from ear to ear, without remorse. Except they are doing this in every season and pigs are only killed once a year, in the autumn, when the weather is cold, just before water freezes. They hang the bodies upside down, bound by the feet, suspended from a tree, and the blood is left to drain out onto the ground. An itinerant bookseller said this.

One man massacres the other over the right to name God. One man slays one man, then, there is retaliation, and five more are slain. Each sect buries its dead in trenches, all together, one body piled on top of another, because there are too many bodies to give each soul its own grave. The foot soldiers of the holy war do not allow firewood to pass through their territory into the towns; there are no trees left to be cut. The wealthy possess furniture to burn, but the poor man, who has already burned his one table and one bench, freezes to death. The warriors are violating women, and the women who survive are left with the hated seed. They are slaying children who are not yet steady on their feet.

They say that Peace, herself, is revolted, and that she holds her stomach and retches; she has hidden her face under a hood and has started to walk away from the battlefields, following along in the ruts made by the wheels of carts, dragging herself along a muddy road that is lined with corpses, not even bothering to lift the hem of her cloak.

This is what the merchant passing through said. We hear things. We hear it in fragments, we hear it in imperfect remnants.

Remnants like the tunic he wears, a *saltimindosso* it is called. Giotto's shepherd wears a *saltimindosso* like this, with a hem torn in three places. The tear must have been recent, otherwise the shepherd would have repaired it, because it is the only garment he possesses. Bartolomeo de Bartolai's shirt is made from clothing discarded from the Signore's villa, a deep black-purple of a fine heavy material. But who is to say this *saltimindosso* is made from a discarded article of clothing? Perhaps it was a blanket that covered his horse.

Each night, he looks at all the irregular pieces and stares at them. A dot, a line, a wave. At times, he has to look away; the pieces seem to be moving, clattering against each other like hundreds of rows of broken teeth.

He scratches his scalp, the discomfort is great.

Even as a child, he got scabs on the top of his head. He would stand with his back to his mother, who sat on the bench and looked through his hair at his scalp. She applied an ointment which she made from beeswax and mint and rosemary and lard. She put this on his scalp in the morning and at night before he went to sleep. She told him the skin of his scalp was drying out, and that his scalp was drying out because his head was too hot from thinking. She asked him again and again about the thoughts inside his head. You have to let your thoughts escape with breath. Otherwise your mind will get too warm, and strange things will begin to happen. As a way of encouraging him to speak, she asked him questions constantly: Do you think it will rain tomorrow? Do you think the frost will come early this year? She would ask him, What are the thoughts bouncing around inside your head? He would try his best to answer her, to describe the thoughts in his head. Why, if the bell tower in Ardonlà blessed by San Bernardino is supposed to keep away storms, why then did the roof of the house called Le Borre collapse? And his mother said, It was from the weight of the snow and it was the will of God. He asked her, If an angel dropped a string from the sky, could you climb to heaven, and, if you could, would your weight pull the angel down? She answered, Angels do not need rope, that is why there is prayer. He asked, Why did the side of the mountain fall into the river and smother the cave with the mosaics? She said, Because the earth has grown heavy and swollen with pride.

In the kitchen, in front of the low stone sink, she grabbed him by the shoulders and shook him, told him not to tell anyone about the sores and not to scratch his scalp in public. Otherwise, they will tell the priest and he will call you before him to ask you what you are thinking. They are burning even humble people at the stake for what they are thinking. When I was a girl, they wanted to execute a miller in Savignano because he was going around saying that the world created itself, that God Himself did not make it. His mind was working too hard; he was burning up with thoughts.

His mother put more salve on his scalp and stopped asking what he was thinking. She asked which plants the sheep had eaten and how many weeds he had pulled from the soil.

Talk, talk, she said to her son, putting ointment on his scalp. Let the heat escape. She urged him to speak, but to not say anything.

꽃

He must not speak, and so he listens. He listens when the priest speaks in church about books, saying how books are like people. How each one is made differently, how some contain holy thoughts, how some contain impure thoughts, how some contain heresy.

The priest says a book is like a human being; it has a spine, and if the book is opened roughly, too quickly, the spine can be snapped, and that a book can scream in pain, yell out, hurl out words, shriek.

A book, he also says, is like fire, and if there are unholy things inside, when the book is closed, the marks on the pages rub against each other, embering twigs, one on top of another, smoldering, burning low as long as the book is closed, and then, the moment the covers are opened, the pages ignite and the book explodes into a ball of fire, singeing the skin and blinding the eyes.

An evil book, he says, can be the Devil himself, taking an elegant, refined form, with the hems of his garments embroidered with gold thread. He can take the form of a book, its covers decorated with fine tooled leather, its pages fluttering like silk. And at night, the priest says, the book changes shape and goes to each of the people sleeping under the roof and puts impure pictures inside their heads so that they dream of sinning in unimagined ways.

He speaks about books in the small round church, even though there is no one present who can read.

※

Bartolomeo de Bartolai cannot read, but he knows this much, that inside a book there are pages. And on those pages are marks. And those who understand the marks get pictures inside their heads. The marks look like vines in spring, brittle and dark, clinging to a wall washed white with lime. He does not understand how to adjust his eyes, the way one does when moving from a field into a forest. In a field, you look for the hare's round shape against the tall straight blades; in the forest you look for a glint of white, the spot on the animal's hind. It is a question of teaching your eyes how to look. This is the secret of understanding a book, he believes, but he does not know how to instruct his eyes.

At night, in the stable, the fragments he has assembled assault his eyes and mock him: This makes no sense, a band of gorse yellow here? Why, Fool?

All the fragments laid out together, separately inarticulate, broken, chipped. It makes him dizzy. It is an untrained swirl, and he becomes so confused he must look away.

⁂

He fans the pieces out carefully.
In one pile, the fragments of blue.

⁂

Giotto's angels tore their hair, clawed the skin of their faces. And he has made three faces like theirs.

He has sketched them out on the panel, and is now forming them with tiles. But on his panel, in his shed, there are not mere angels. The top one is a god, who, like the Signore, is the most powerful. The one in the middle is a god who is the next most powerful and is his heir. Below him is another god who is the least powerful, but has other powers the other two do not, because he is also light. Bartolomeo de Bartolai has made three gods; he believes they are three and distinct and separate, each having his place in the hierarchy.

He believes he has made a picture that is holy and sacred, but if the ambitious priest were to hear of it, a priest who wants to escape from the mountains and be allowed to return to the plains, Bartolomeo de Bartolai would be interrogated. Why have you drawn this, my son? You do not really mean to say that God is three different beings? The priest would turn to Bartolomeo de Bartolai, ask him to renounce the work, to redefine it, reminding him that God is one and indivisible. That God created light. That God is not light.

He shows the panel to no one, not because he considers this dissent, but because it is a peasant's habit to conceal. For the cheeks, he has saved his most precious glass, pieces of Asian porcelain tinted pink.

It is nearly winter. No one passes through on the narrow road above. Snow has already fallen. Bartolomeo de Bartolai tells himself he must admit what is obvious, that Giotto is ancient and it is unlikely he will travel up into these mountains.

He returns to the stable each night, crossing the *ara*. He hangs the lantern on a wooden peg, burns the precious oil. He throws the goat Diana a piece of crust he has saved. He stares at the dried-out board of pine, dreams of pictures he has seen before. He is no longer waiting for the great man. Great men do not arrive. He will never go down out of the mountains. He will soothe the foreheads of his elders, and the past will be his future.

Bartolomeo de Bartolai sits on the ground on clean straw under a dim yellow light, his fingers aching with cold. He fans out the pieces before him. He examines his few shards of cobalt and azurite blue. He begins to set them in mastic, though he has not collected sufficient fragments to complete the sky.

The Child Carrier

sit up. Hold the holy medals still, flat against my breast so they do not tinkle. They are warm. Put one leg over the edge of the bed. My foot flat on the cold floor. Put the other foot down flat. My ankles are thin again. It was the sight of my ankle, he said.

My empty house shoes. How does that riddle go again? *Èd nott' son voda—Ed giòren son pina. Gran dutòur è chi gh'indovina.* During the day I'm full, and at night I'm emptied. Whoever guesses this riddle is a smart doctor indeed.

Shoes.

Stupid riddle. I slip my feet into my house shoes.

✂

I arch each foot inside the shoe and grip it so the shoes do not clap against the floor, and I step slowly. At the foot of the bed the cradle. Black curls under the bonnet. The longer he sleeps the better. I will have two babies to manage. I move quietly toward the bedroom door.

She will bring her baby over to me at seven. Is she saying her good-byes now? Does she care? Get rid of it. She must. It is not a very pretty baby. And the father?

But she has suffered, too, her husband dying like that, three small children. No help from his family. Her family yes, but what do they have? Less than we have. And what do we have?

✳

In the kitchen, I open the shutters and look out. Black. The birds are not awake yet. Not the chickens either.

The baggage is next to the door. I bathed the older two last night. All I have to do is feed myself, the baby, the girls, him. Dress myself, the girls, the baby. My sister will come to get the girls this morning before I go so they are not alone when I leave.

I have never been to an inn. They are paying, but what if they end up taking it out of my pay? It could be nice but it could be dirty, like the one over in Barigazzo.

✳

I am carrying a baby down, down out of the mountains, into the plains to the sea. To Viareggio, where the second mother with another wet nurse will take him from my arms and give me the rest of the money to give to the first mother.

Three days the trip should take if all goes well. Giovanna from Moradina says there is another baby to take if I want. That one to Ferrara. To *signori* in Ferrara.

✳

As long as I am nursing, I cannot get pregnant.

My breasts are sore this morning.

The baby has a tooth beginning.

⁂

He said my hands are rough. Is it my fault?

Enough. I do not want to start crying again. Both times, after the girls, too, yes, but this is different. Deeper. I don't know if it will end. The midwife says it passes, the dark period at the end of pregnancy, yes, but this is different from the other times. The other times, if I kept busy every second, it would lift up sometimes for a moment. This? This is different.

Licia's hands are shaped like mine. Lidia, no.

⁂

I'll have an egg. Whip it up in a glass. Drink it. Strengthen my nerves.

I wait to hear the baby cooing. Angel baby.

⁂

Out the window, it is still dark. Clouds. No rain, I hope. I would like to see the views. I have only been that way once before, only as far as Barga. For the fair one time with my father and brother. He bought my mother a silk scarf with a design of morning glories and poppies.

⁂

In some places, they say, the road is hardly visible.

It was washed away this spring in certain places when the snow melted and in the rain. By now the roads should have been repaired in those places. But who knows? They can assure you, assure you, assure you, but when you get there and the road is difficult to pass you have to go forward. They won't pay me if I turn around and come back.

In certain places, the road was washed out in the mud slides, at the Passo del Radici and in a stretch before Castiglione. A driver said the other day that the road had been fixed, but who do you trust? With an infant in each arm, I'll trust myself.

When the snow melted, there was so much rain, and the river rose. We hung lanterns on the branches of the poplar trees along the side of the river, and we watched from higher up on the mountainside. It was black like pitch and the lanterns looked like a strand of beads. The roar from the river sounded like I don't know what, not like an earth tremor, but more like breathing, like a giant breathing. Like a giant with water in his lungs breathing.

We watched all night from up above town. One lantern went out, then another. The river was rising and the flames were starting to go out. It is a flood, we all thought. Two more lights went out. Letizia Pini started to wail; her house is close to the bank. Other lanterns went out and everyone stood there staring down. It was black, and you could not hear what anyone was saying because of the roar. There were some who stood around the priest and prayed, but most of the others stood to one side with their arms folded and looked down. I thought the town would be submerged, but then, after those few lanterns went out, that was the end of it; they must have gone out because of the wind or because the water was leaping up from the river. When daylight started to show, most of the lanterns were still lit, and the water was going down.

Even though the roads were ruined in certain places, they kept pushing me to come sooner, as if I have any control over the seasons, as if I were making up stories about the roads. At the end of May, the midwife sent word to her that it wasn't passable, that it wasn't safe to come down yet. She sent word back, and you would have thought she had been swindled. That I was not going to honor the contract. Doesn't she understand that things are out of my control, the weather, the sun and the moon? This is the soonest I can go, and she understands nothing about it.

This morning, it is cold again. We are still burning wood in the fireplace. The season is a month late already. It is damp and drizzling.

O Cimone, I know you're out there in the dark, you old tired mountain. What have you got to say for yourself today?

My mother was hired as a wet nurse, just like her mother, just like I am now. My grandmother went away, down from the mountains to Prato, and she stayed there at the hospital for one year. She left her children, including my uncle who was a baby and the last to be born, with her sister, who nursed him along with her own son.

They used to leave their unwanted infants at the door of the hospital, she said. It was a revolving door, like a wheel; *la ruota,* it was called, and the infant would be left outside in this door late at night or early in the morning, and the child could be taken in without the identity of the person leaving the baby being known.

They left babies whose mothers could not give them milk, babies whose mothers were dead, babies whose parents wanted a boy instead of a girl, babies of prostitutes, babies of mothers who were not wed, babies of widows, babies of mothers and fathers who could not support them. In France, they had the same thing, *la ruota,* but much later, and never in England or in Spain. In Portugal, yes. Many times, she said, the infants died in the wheel.

Death boxes she called those hospitals. Better to die, exposed on the side of a mountain. They died just the same, but on the side of the mountain they died sooner and suffered less.

✄

The parents, once they left their child behind, could not know anything more, unless they wanted to reclaim the child. They would try sometimes, my grandmother said, to contact the wet nurse, to ask about their child.

She told me this, that the infants left in the revolving door were never left there naked. They were wrapped up and warm. They were wrapped in wool, or cotton, or linen. When the babies arrived, she said, their heads were almost always covered and protected.

✄

For a year, my grandmother left her children with her sister. The hospital did not allow a wet nurse to bring her own infant with her. For a year, she gave her milk to nineteen different babies. Ten of the children she nursed died. The mother of one little boy came back. She gave her milk to nineteen babies but not to her own son who was nursed by her sister.

They paid her each month and she sent the money to her sister. At the end of the year, when her contract was finished, they paid her another sum, and when she came home, she divided it with her sister.

They paid her to embroider, too. They paid her to sort the straw that was used to make hats.

Every few months, a nun would write a card for her and sign her name, with the message, *In Christ peace. Your mother.*

The babies were left with little signs to show who they were. There were ribbons. A ribbon of a certain color. How did my grandmother explain it again?

The babies came in with little signs. Many would have a half of a coin tucked in with their clothing. The coin was broken in two so that in the future, parent and child would be able to recognize each other.

And they left notes. Notes that said, *Angelina, I will come back to get you. Your mother.* That said, *Carolina, it is with a heavy heart that I must leave you here because I am in utter desperation due to a fate over which I have no control our Lord who is in his infinite wisdom has taken my beloved your mother Renata to be with him. I do not want to leave you here but I will come back for you Your father Anselmo.*

Please, out of charity take this child.

Please, call this child Battista. He has been baptized.

Please, her name is Ma. Grazia.

These children were called by various names. *Abbandonati. Esposti. Trovatelli. Gettatelli.* Abandoned, exposed, found, thrown away infants.

I can only do what I can do. He says I make everything too hard. Think too much. What is there to this? Go down, deliver her baby, come back.

What is her choice? She can't feed the others, let alone this one.

I just take the baby down to the sea. Down past Barga. Past Lucca, to the sea, and there, hand the baby over to someone who is waiting, who will take the baby away. The family has a farm in France, and the wife cannot have a child. They are waiting for this one. The child has a name and has been baptized, but they will probably rename him.

※

Moses was abandoned but he was destined to be found.

This poor little child is fortunate, too. She found someone to take him; she found a buyer.

※

This morning I will have some camomile when it is light and the girls are awake. Lidia likes to stand against my leg while I am sitting at the table. She asks me to let her put her cheek against the warm cup.

I will be gone three days. Maybe less, maybe more. I should be in a village near Lucca by dark. We will spend the night there at an inn, then take another carriage to Lucca, then a train from there to Viareggio. The sixteenth of June is the animal market down in the big field and I will be back home in time.

※

He said to me when I took this work, Why do you have to take along the baby, my son? Leave him here. Leave him with your sister. For two days he can drink goat milk; it's not going to kill him, he's a strong boy. Or leave him with Menga; Michele owes me money. She will keep him for a few days.

No, I said to him. No, I will not leave my son, your son, with anyone. He is coming with me when I go down to Viareggio to hand over the other one. Summer is here and stomach diseases start now, I told him. He's got a strong heart, but no, I am not going to leave him behind, I don't care what you say. A baby needs his mother's milk. Maybe it seems to you that three days is nothing, but I say, no, he's better off making the trip with me, even if it is a difficult trip. Besides that little what's-her-name from town is going to be making the same trip and she will help me take care of the two babies.

What lungs though, when he starts to cry. There will be two babies in a closed carriage. I hope the driver does not put us out somewhere on the side of the road.

In the end, how much help will that what's-her-name be? Probably not much. But she can't help it, growing up without a mother and her aunts busy with their own. They found her a household in Genoa, going to work in the house of a shoe merchant.

I've never been past Bagni di Lucca. Once as far as Barga with my father. My brother and father and I went. And he bought a silk scarf and thread for my mother.

The little ones, my grandmother said, were almost always left with a token, with some kind of sign their parents sent with them, tucked into their clothing. The tokens were attached to ribbons or strips of cloth that held medals and coins, some false, but mainly they were legitimate coins that had been broken in two. Broken in two and attached to a ribbon or a strip of cloth and tucked in with the infant's clothing. And along the edge of the coin where it had been broken, there would be a jagged and worn-down ridge, and you could run a finger across the edge where it was broken, where the pieces could be fit together.

They were signs so that the parent and child could recognize each other. Coins. Crosses and pieces of crosses. Scarves and pieces of coral. An earring, a cuff link, a clasp. There were small sacks filled with small objects: a stamp, a bell, a link from a chain, half of a button, a flower, a pig's tooth.

The notes and objects were listed in a big book, she said. The book and the objects were kept under lock and key, and mainly no one reclaimed the objects, which were never shown to the children.

What will she pack with her baby? Something? Anything? A ribbon tied around his wrist, a key, a piece of paper with his name. It would be foolishness, useless. Those items would not be kept. Why should they be? The child will never know her as a mother. He will know another mother; he will not even know her language. Why send a token? Why would it be saved? It does not matter; the child will have a life, perhaps a whole life if he is lucky.

Maybe she will send a press-dried sprig of campanula. A sprig of rosemary for remembrance.

But why? Why burden someone with having to decide whether to throw these objects away or to save them?

It ends here, the minute she places the infant in my hands, and I step into the carriage and roll away with him from Ardonlà.

But what if the infant lives to become a child, and discovers, perhaps, from a jeering cousin, from a comment by a teacher, that he is connected, not to the mother he knows, but to another one. And he rushes into the stomach of the mother he has always known, saying,

What are they talking about? They are saying you are not my real mother. Would the only mother he has ever known want to say, You see, she could not care for you; she was not able to care for you, and she gave you to me because she could not feed you. No she did not throw you away. She did not want to give you away, but she had to. Look, look, come upstairs, I will show you here in this cupboard, in this tin box, here, this is something she tucked into your blankets.

On the top shelf of the cupboard in the wall, behind the glass door on the right, there is a white soup tureen with a cover. There is a green stripe painted around the lid. The dish has a crack down the side, but the crack is turned away from the glass, and the bowl is something fine to look at. The postcards the nuns wrote for my grandmother are in the bowl, under the lid. There are five of them, stacked one on top of the other. Four are the same, a picture of the Madonna standing on top of the world, and the other one is the child Jesus wearing his little round hat and his cloak with jewels and giving a blessing with two fingers pointed up.

And my brother's picture is there on the cupboard door, in the bottom left corner between the glass and the wooden frame. He is wearing a suit and a tie. Egidio, my baby brother. One of his legs is crossed over the other, and his hands are folded on his knee, and you can still see how calm he is. The picture was made in a photographer's studio in Colorado, but now he is in a place called Dawson, New Mexico, and they say there are mountains there, too, but different from ours, empty and without trees, and dry like the desert. I am afraid he will die inside a mountain, like others who have gone to America.

I scraped my knuckles washing a sheet on a rock in the river. It was a rough rock, sandstone, and it must have been thrown in by someone upstream, because it was not smooth like a river stone. When I move my hand in a certain way, open and close it, every so often, the scab cracks opens a bit.

Listen to the rain. And last year, nothing.

I was hoping for a beautiful summer day, to be able to see far-away views. Instead, there will be clouds and fog.

Listen to the rain come down. The roads will be mud. It will take three times as long to get down to the plains. The new mother has threatened that she will find another child if this one does not arrive soon.

The road is paved only near the bigger towns and at difficult passes. There are no walls on the side of the road, except at the bridges and certain curves. Will we need to get out and walk? We will pass mules carrying loads and peasants walking behind their herds. For centuries and centuries, shepherds have been taking their flocks down into the Maremma. They leave in September and return in May. And now, I am taking the baby down out of the mountains, along with the other exports, lumber, livestock, chestnuts, charcoal.

He wants me to leave the baby Egidio behind but I will not. He made it through winter without a problem breathing, without pneumonia or bronchitis. When babies die in the winter, it is because their breathing is disrupted and they cannot take in enough air. Now, he wants me to leave the baby behind, now that I've gotten him through the winter, and leave him open to the stomach sicknesses. I will not do it, leave him for a few days to someone else. It is my milk that makes him strong. How do I know he would take someone else's milk, or that they won't feed him goat milk instead? In the mountains, babies die mostly in the winter months. On the plains and in the city, they say, they die in the summer from diseases in the stomach.

Mostly the infants were abandoned in April and May, my grandmother said, after the hard winter and before the hard work of summer.

In some places nine out of ten died. They died from the journey. Some had never had a mother's milk. Many died in the wheel itself, but this one will not, nor will mine. There are new bridges and roads. Both babies are strong.

Will this trip at such an early age make my son a wanderer? Will he get a taste of the outside world, of the world down there, too soon, and leave, never come back?

In the summer we are all together. In the winter, he is gone, gone with the men working. This summer he is here again. We are all together.

He does not want me to take this infant down to the city, but I said, are we so well off that we can afford to pass up this money? He set his jaw like a metal trap.

But enough is enough. Last winter, we went for weeks with nothing but dried-out tree-bread, bread made from chestnut flour, and a few pieces of cheese, and *polenta* with nothing on top, waiting for the money to arrive, while he was down in the plains, eating enough, seeing the world. I told him, We do not have enough to pass this up. I think that for a few days you should be able to make do without me; I do without you for six months. He looked at me like he could not believe I had said it, as if to say, I liked the old sweet Ímola better. It was my moment to speak up and I did. I said, You cannot expect me to take care of everything for half of the year, the children, the land, the house, the firewood, the needlework I sell to the nuns, you can't expect me to do all this, and then, the second you step back through the door, to become a lamb. I said it. I should not have said it. He turned away and walked out. I know what he did. I know he walked down to Le Rive and saw Mirandola. I know. I know. I know. I bury it all and am dumb again; but I will go down to the sea first.

He does not strike me, he does not strike the children, but he is a cruel man. Even when he has been drinking, he does not raise his hand and only rarely raises his voice. His cruelty is silence. Like the face of that mountain out there.

The other night I dreamed that he touched my right nipple and inside I contracted and expanded. The sheet was moist, but he had not touched me, and his back was a flat scarp of granite.

I lie down at night; there is one less night of sleep left. When did I begin to think in this way? Have I always thought this way? For the first time I think, What if I had married Bartolomeo instead. A sin to think these things? But Bartolomeo is who-knows-where. In South

America? And if I had gone with him, no one would remember me anymore. Ímola? Yes. I vaguely recall her. Tall with thin ankles and hazel eyes, but I don't remember anything else about her.

And his body in the bed is so far away from me at night; he hoards his body warmth. In the day, he says nothing to me in the fewest words possible.

My life is passing before my eyes, like a dream. I try to take account of it at night in bed but fall asleep exhausted. The fatigue. Then wake up again, wide awake.

Last night, I felt my cheek flat against the sheets, which were clean and stiff and cool. Pounded against the rocks and washed in the stream. On the pillow cases, as a girl, I embroidered my initials; who was that person with those other initials? He sleeps on a pillow covered by a clean pillow case and will not reach out a hand to me.

At the fair in September he kissed me. Quickly, in the dark. There was light from the bonfire in the field. And when he spoke you could see his breath rising into the sky.

His eyes were like jewels that burned through my bone. His eyes are the green of a precious stone, like a cat's eye, like a gem that sends back light in the same direction it comes from, that reflects from within.

He knows things I do not know and I trust his judgment.

In the fall, he will go away again, with a group going down close to Rome, where they are building a road. He is going to haul rocks for the masons.

⚜

With this baby, I lost another tooth, the one on the bottom to the left of the center teeth. A tooth for every child, they say, but I have lost only two and have three children alive.

They say that in India there are slaves and the children some-times escape from their masters, who chain them by the ankle while the children weave carpets.

In Ethiopia, they say that boys with legs like sticks and heads like skulls travel in packs and that they learn their letters in the desert by writing them with sticks in the red dirt.

In Paris, they say that people bring children to sell to rich people and that the merchants who sell them get rich, but that there are always more babies for sale than people who want them and the orphanages are full.

I bore them, but he named them. The two girls and the baby. The girls Licia and Lidia; the names are similar but they are not twins.

Those people who left behind their babies sometimes packed food and medicine in with the babies. Butter and herbs to help the babies sleep. They put pieces of coral in with the babies to protect them. Red or white coral to calm a storm or to help a person who is crossing a river.

This morning, like so many mornings, I could not sleep and woke up hours and hours before dawn.

I wake up when I should be sleeping. I need the strength. But instead I wake up and all different things are in my head. Thoughts come from every direction, from up higher in the mountains and from down below, they drop from the sky and come up from the earth.

This morning, I woke up from a dream. The dream was this, that he had taken his hunting dog away somewhere in the direction of Lama Mocogno, and there was a fire that started at the fair in the field where horses were being sold, and he left his hunting dog behind; then, when he came back home he did not even try to explain that he had lost the dog. And in the dream, at the same moment the fire was burning in the field, I was away in the other direction, and I was carrying a bundle in my arms. It was not that it was heavy to carry, although it wasn't light either, but mainly it was difficult to manage because it was so large. I had crumpled it into a ball, and as I carried it, one corner would escape from my arms. I would shove it back into the ball, but another part would come out. It was a tablecloth of white linen which I had been working for months and months, embroidering the hem and the middle. In the city, I set the bundle down near a fountain, and when I left I forgot I had set it down. But then much later, when I remembered, I ran back to get it. And when I got back to the fountain, there was a bundle there, an embroidered tablecloth, but it wasn't mine. The needlework was poor and the stuff was not of good quality either.

This is the dream I woke up with, and I laid there for a while but sleep would not come back. So I got up, and here I am now sitting in a chair at the window staring at the black sky.

⚜

We are in a valley up here. In these parts, there are no towns up higher.

From here, the roads out of the mountains go off in three different directions. They go down to the city of Modena, down to Florence through the pass at Abetone, and down to Lucca. From here, going in three directions, they must attach teams of horses to help pull the carriages and carts up the steep roads. In some places the roads are very narrow and there is a sheer drop. The teams of horses pull them up as far as the passes.

We are in a valley high up in the mountains, and in order to descend into the plains, you first have to climb up higher.

⁂

I know the other roads, but I do not know the road to Lucca. I went on it only one time as a girl when my father bought the scarf for my mother. We will ride all day and stop at night near Lucca. From the inn, they will take me to the train station in Lucca, Giovanna told me. She says it is easy, the only thing is that there are so many people and so much noise. She says to give the driver a little extra money when I pay him, and after he gets the bags down to ask him to take us to the track where the train for Viareggio is sitting. He will either be a compassionate type who will see you with two babies and help you or he will be rude and bark. But if you give him some money, she said, either way, he will get you to the right train.

She said to ignore the confusion. There will be people running and shouting. I will not see anything of Lucca or Viareggio either. No time. She says to keep to myself, to pack enough food, and water to drink. There are places to eat along the way, but they will cost money and be dirty, and the men in there will make rude comments. She said to stay in the carriage when it stops, and to not let the little girl out of my sight because she is a flirt and doesn't know what she is doing.

⁂

The time we went to Barga, I remember, we went to Mass on Sunday. The three of us stood in the back of the church because there were no seats left. I got tired of standing and my father would not let me lean against the wall. In front, there was a statue of St. Christopher, with Christ up on his shoulder. I remember I asked my father to pick me up, but he said I was too old for that.

I'm too late for narcissus and wild tulips, too early for the lilies. Maybe somewhere along the way there will be rhododendrons in bloom, climbing up the side of a mountain. But everything is late this year; maybe they won't open at all. Above the road, past the road that goes to the monastery, there is a big forest of beech trees. And above the line where the forest ends, there is nothing but gravel and sheer rock. Maybe we will stop somewhere and I will lay the babies down in a field of nard; it smells like perfume. Will acacia be blooming down closer to the sea?

I could not sleep and woke up thinking about blind beggars in the city, the wrong train. That no one one will understand when I speak. That my clothes will mark me and I will be mocked. That bandits will come up from nowhere and steal from me, drive away the carriage. No, no, those are old stories. There are no bandits anymore; there is safety on the road, except when a horse stumbles at a difficult pass or a rock falls from above.

These are the things I woke up thinking about. These things and leaving the girls. And taking my baby. And handing over the other one to strangers. And him going God-knows-where for his pleasure.

Mô guarda, l'é semper un bell'uomo. Look. He is still a handsome man.

My shoulders are starting to round. I must keep them straight. If not, I'll end up like my aunt, hunched over young.

⁂

I have never been out of the mountains, never been to the plains or seen the Mediterranean. These are things I know nothing about.

Giovanna has made this trip before; she said there is nothing to worry about. But I have seen many leave who do not come back. They went to Brazil, they went to America in Colorado, in Texas, in Illinois. Some went to Russia. Two brothers went to Mozambique. My mother's cousin, the tall one, went to Africa. They all go out and down and away, and they say they will come back, but they just disappear. I am going out, down, away. I will come back in a few days, but still it makes me afraid. If I fall off the face of the earth, who will remember me?

The Coal Loader, Above Ground

All day long, the hares hide in depressions in the ground, in any ruts they can find, trying to stay out of the sun, and in the late afternoon, they start to move around, eating those plants that they eat.

Sometimes, after my work at the mines is done, I walk east on the road with my shotgun. On both sides is the plain. Then, after four miles, I turn to the south and I walk another mile. I find a bush, kick it, and watch. Then I walk some more, kick a bush, and watch. You have to wait a long time because a jackrabbit has ears like a deer and can hear any sound; he has eyes that can see five miles away.

All around there are snakeweed plants with woody stems, three feet tall, sometimes as tall as a man, and at the end of each branch, there are hundreds of flowers in clusters. They are done blooming now, in October, and are brown. But here and there, a spot of yellow.

There is no movement out on the plain, but soon the animals will start showing themselves, start looking for their supper. The sun is getting lower. The only motion is up above, a circling turkey hawk.

⚘

Outside town, to the east, is the cemetery, which I passed walking here and I will pass going back. On the graves, there are hills of red ants.

To the east of here, from where I walk now, the land is completely flat, except for some buttes that stick out like thumbs. And farther east, on the horizon, there is a mesa that runs for miles and looks like a piece of strung-out rope.

Behind me to the west, back beyond town, the plain collides with a mesa. Behind the mesa there are hills that are black and coral red. And beyond the hills are the mountains, the Sangue di Cristo, which go north into Colorado and south down toward Taos. The mountains are a day away. All around me, there are dried-out rifts in this red clay. I look out and see only cattle and wire fences and runty plants.

All this I would write to you all if I could. Instead, my friend, Antenore, has written these words on postcards for me: *Vi ricordo tutti.* I remember you all. And I sign my name. Bartolai, Egidio.

⚘

The ground is mainly sandstone and clay. The earth is rust. The bed of the river is red, and they call the river Vermijo, which now, in the fall, is a trickle, drier than spit. In the spring, the water comes down in torrents from the hills; it comes so fast that it fills the riverbed up above the banks. A flood can take less than ten minutes, and any-

87

thing in its path, a grown man with his trouser legs rolled up and washing his feet, is swept away.

Near town, down along the river, there is tall salt grass. Along the shore, there is a stand of cottonwoods, and this is one of the few places where there is a wide strip of shade. The shore of the river is clay that is hard-packed and the color of rust, and children sit there and make little figures and bowls with the clay. They take their items out in the sun and place them to dry on the stones that line the path that goes from the river to town. When they dry, they are very fragile and crumble as soon as they are touched.

There is a mule path that follows the river away from town and goes up into higher ground. Up in that direction a mile are four pine trees, and they call the settlement there *I Pini,* a hamlet of people who don't want to live in town and have bought a little piece of scrubland.

The town is set up on a mound, a quarter mile to the north of the river. It seems too far back when you see there is no water in the river this time of year. Up the road from town, about a mile, up against the mesa, is the mine, with its tipple and chute.

This is what I would tell you, all of this.

Siamo vicino al confine di New Mexico *e* Colorado.

This is what I would tell you. We are near the border of New Mexico and Colorado.

This is what I would have Antenore write for me: *C'è un treno che viene dal nord, attraversando il paese di* Raton, New Mexico. *Per arrivare qui a* Stag Canyon Coal Company, *si viaggia una distanza di trenta miglie da* Raton *e si arriva ad un* saloon *operato da un americano.*

I would tell you: There is a train that comes from the north and passes through Raton, New Mexico. To arrive here at the Stag Canyon Coal Company, you travel thirty miles south from Raton and arrive at a saloon operated by an American. At the saloon, you leave the main line and take another train for five miles.

This is how you arrive at the end at Dawson.

᠅

The first time I came, I came down on a train from Denver, through Trinidad, Colorado. It was winter, and when the train came to the highest part of the Raton pass, it slowed. On either side of the train, the rock was red and brown, the color of a scab. There were patches of snow. Above, you could see the road; it was one curve after another. It looked like it was chiseled into the stone, and there was a man walking in front of a mule. There were a few trees, junipers, pine trees and oak, but mainly it was rock. After we came through the pass, there was a valley with the town of Raton. There was a cloud of black smoke above it and the odor of coal stung.

᠅

Off in the distance, a train goes north to Colorado, beyond Raton. Antenore has gone up there to make trouble. He is looking for trouble. He left cursing me. Antenore, with his books.

᠅

I carry the gun in my hand at my side and kick the dry red ground. The stray dog has followed me out here. I call him Capron' because he has short white wiry fur like a goat. He moves in broad circles, trots, like he is looking for something.

᠅

Every season, when the weather changes, I think, What would it be like over there at this particular moment? I imagine the shape of the mountains at home. The colors in each season. In winter, grey. Then green. Then gold.

Last year, I thought I would be back there by this time, by autumn.

Last year, I thought I would be back there to gather mushrooms. Now I think about the spring, and when spring comes, I will think about the fall. Four years have gone.

I ask myself, What would I do when I got there?

Leave again.

※

There is a place I go every year to gather mushrooms in the mountains at home; I follow a long ridge up past the stone hut the barbarians built; follow it to a grove of pine trees. At the south end of the grove, three days after the first rain in June, there are always mushrooms there.

From August until November, you can find the mushroom called *trombetta da morto,* the death trumpet. Sometimes, it is called the cornucopia. The mushroom is grey. There is a grove of beech trees halfway up Monte Cimone where you can always find some.

There are harvests going to waste. I thought of telling someone, my sister, Ímola, maybe, but then, if I had, when I go back, it would no longer be my spot.

Now, when I think about the mountains at home, even the rain and the fog seem like food. I think about the color green and looking out at hill after hill, so thick you can see nothing underneath. In a forest you hear things, you do not see them. A rabbit hitting against a branch. Here, there is nothing to hit against. You can see a deer a mile away, there is no place for it to hide. Creatures come up from under the ground, stick their long necks out, look around, then disappear down into a hole. The cactus is so confused it doesn't know which way to grow; it starts in one direction, then twists itself into another.

※

A labor recruiter came up into the mountains. He said that in America there would be work in the mines in the winter and fall, and in the spring and summer there would be work in the fields. He said, Don't come back for at least five years, otherwise you can't make the journey pay. Out west there is land for sale cheap, he said, in the Middle West, in Illinois and Indiana and Iowa, there is no land left, it is already owned by Germans. But in the West, there is unclaimed land, and they have sheep and cattle that thrive in the desert. It is not, he said, a desert like Africa, but a desert with mountains where bushes that flower grow. There is an abundance of wildlife, hares and pheasants and deer, he said.

※

Every morning, I pass by a hut at the entrance to the mine and show my badge, a small brass circle with a number, and the mine official marks me down. Number three hundred and ninety-two.

I walk into the elevator cage that goes down the shaft into the mine. It is a cage that holds forty men, ten on each level. I step in with nine others, and it is lowered six feet to let another group in above us. You hear their feet shuffle against the metal. Except for the strip of light on the side of the cage that comes from the top of the shaft, it is all blackness. The cage jerks and is dropped six more feet, and another

91

ten miners get in. And again. Forty men and the cage is lowered down into the shaft. I hold my lunch pail and adjust my cap. As I go down, to clear my ears, I swallow.

The mine is three thousand feet deep. All around the cage, the shaft is coal black. The metal cables groan as they are wound over the drum.

At the bottom, the lamp of a miner's cap throws off light for twenty feet; past that, it is darkness.

Some say they prefer it down in the mine to up above. They come to believe that the air above is no good, and that the air in the coal mine is pure.

When I get out of the mine at the end of the day, I want to forget about the mine, I want to forget about how dark it is, how quiet it is.

Every morning, I dig out my shovel and pick from under the mound where I hid them the night before. I lift up my pick. At first it seems impossible to start, to take one swing, when the coal car is empty. Each morning, I think, I don't have enough strength to start up, to move coal from one place to another. I swing at the wall. And after the first break, then the second, the body loosens, and the movement keeps itself going, and you break and lift and carry.

In the coal, you can see the imprint of creatures and plants that were living then, before the coal was coal, when it was a swamp. Millions and millions of years ago. There were streams that deposited silt and dirt. Leaves fell to the bottom of the water and were pressed down by the weight of other living things falling on top, and this is how the coal was formed.

In the seam, one time, I saw a frond as tall as me, and, once, I found an animal's tooth.

⚹

With one hundred men working on the same level, some of them in nearby rooms, you would think you would hear voices often, but the coal in the walls smothers sound. All you hear is yourself working. Even the sound of the first piece of coal being dropped into the empty car is just a thud with no echo.

⚹

I sometimes stop working for a moment and I am not surrounded by the sounds of my body moving, the shovel scraping against the floor, the cloth of one pants leg rubbing against the other. In this silence, there are sometimes sounds. A timber, bending from the weight above it, creaks. Sometimes in the silence, there is a sound that seems like water trickling down the face of rock, like a place in the mountains where water slides down in a thin sheet. It makes a tinkling sound that tickles the eardrum. In the mine, though, that sound is not water; it is gas seeping, and you have to find it and burn it out with your lamp; you have to plug the place where it is leaking, or it will explode.

⚹

In the late afternoon when I come back up, I step outside the cage, then walk outside the exit, and the first thing I see is the sun glinting off the metal roof of the hut where I show my badge. The

93

sunlight stings, and it is hard to believe this is not the brightest time of the day. The sun behind me has still not dropped, and to the north, the mesa is not yet in shadow. Five hundred leave the mine. Men ahead of me and behind me talk, but the first thing I listen for is the sound of the crickets.

※

This summer the mine will close down, and they say there may be work at the Harding mine in Dixon. They don't dig coal there; they dig up crystals that look like emeralds.

In our part of the mountains at home, there is nothing inside the mountain but gravel and rock. That stone called Apennine *macigno* which is grey and hard as granite but shatters easily. It is not like the mountains down near Montecatini where there is copper, or near Carrara where there is marble. At home, there is nothing to pull out of those rocks, nothing but more rock.

※

Antenore said that the mountain people, in the days before the Romans, were nomads, travelling from one zone to another, up into the mountains in the spring, down onto the plains in the fall. Shepherds, migrating, who did not have a language that could be written down or read. This is what Antenore said. Antenore, with his books, who believes he is some great thinker. Up north, making trouble.

Antenore who was in love with my sister. He brought her a bunch of flowers one time. He made her laugh, but she turned him away because he was two years younger. Then, she married Achille. Achille, who everyone knew was still following after another woman.

※

I send postcards to my sister, Ímola, for the rest of the family. I send them postcards of places I have not seen. Only of the high country, none of the desert. There was one that showed a mountain coming straight out from the plain, like a wall, with no foothills. There was one of a canyon with a cliff a mile tall on each side. In town, they sell a postcard with a picture of the coal mine and the name of the company written on it. I did not send them that one, but postcards of other places. Of beautiful places.

I intend to send a postcard more often but there is too much to say and I cannot say it.

One time, I sent a postcard with an Indian hut. The Indians live nowhere nearby; they live to the south on the other side of the mountains. The photo reminded me of a charcoalmaker's hut back in the mountains at home. The Indians' hut was made of mud and stone, with long poles leaning up against it. There were two girls standing in front. One was taller than the other, and they both had their hands folded in front of them. I thought of my nieces, Licia and Lidia, who would be eight and six by now.

I remember I held Licia on my lap. She put her little hand on my shoulder. Then she put her hands on my cheeks and put her face up close to mine and said to me, Uncle, the moon is asleep; it's sleeping on its side.

I have never met the boy because he was born after I left. My sister sent me a postcard after he was born. It said everyone was fine, except for my father. It said the baby was strong and they gave my name to him, Egidio, after the saint who performed many miracles in a forest, according to those who believe.

❦

Once, while I was hunting, I saw an animal off in the distance that looked something like an antelope and something like a deer. He had wandered down onto the plain from the mountains. His body was brown and his belly was white; he was sleek. His face was like a goat's. His horns were short, each shaped like a horseshoe with points, with several points, like fingers on a hand. I watched him. He ate, then looked up. Ate, then looked up. When he moved to a different bush, I raised my gun. I fired but I missed, and he ran away; he was the fastest creature I have ever seen. He disappeared to the north in a second.

I walked to the place where he had been grazing. He had been eating sagebrush. I looked down at the ground at his tracks and saw that his hind hooves were much smaller than his front hooves. I thought to myself that his prints were shaped like a heart split down the middle.

❦

I do not think I meant to come away this far. I did not know how big this country was and, in my mind, Illinois was close to Texas, Alabama was close to Colorado. I thought the sea was the great distance. I knew this country was vast, but I could not imagine the distance between two places.

I left because I wanted to feel bold; because I felt bold for a moment. In the mountains, everyone leaves for somewhere, for Switzerland, for Sardegna, for the Maremma, but the bold ones come here. I saw how old man Rasponi's sons sent money back from America; I saw how he bought a new field. I saw how when his son Olinto returned, men made a circle around him and no one interrupted him when he spoke. He said that anyone can go down to Grossetto, down to the Maremma, but a bold man crosses the ocean. I remember how Amedeo Contri grabbed Olinto's shirt; he wanted to fight. Olinto pushed him away like a gnat, then pulled out his pipe and started to smoke.

⚜

We came over in a group of four, me and Antenore from Ardonlà, Raimondo Marchioni and Angelo Lolgli from Fiumalbo. Marchioni is in Illinois and Lolgli went up to work in a copper mine in Utah.

Now, Antenore is up in Colorado. There is a newspaper there, *La Luce,* and he wants to write articles about the worker. Antenore, with his books and pamphlets. Manzoni. Malatesta. Engels. He left with his suitcase and his big dictionary. Up to Colorado where there is trouble. The miners are on strike; the owners have brought in the army. They are killing miners up there, but we stay quiet here.

⚜

I look out over all this dryness. When the wind blows hard we put scarves over our mouths and try to get inside. The dust chokes the old men. My father would not survive an hour. The dirt blows; it is not like dirt that is black or brown. It is silt when it covers your skin. And when it hardens, it is like clay.

⚜

There are some who want to organize this mine, bring down the miners' federation from Colorado. We have a good mine here. They brought in a doctor from Oklahoma. They built a washhouse near the exit. The union sent down men from Colorado, but the company would not allow them in. The guards fired shots above their heads, and they ran away like rabbits. They say that up north, the capitalists are afraid for the miners to have guns and that a man cannot keep a gun for hunting.

Up in Pueblo, Colorado, they lynched three Italians.

Better to keep your head down.

Even when they taunt you, it's better to stay still.

In Raton, I was in a saloon. I was standing at the bar with Antenore. An American miner, a drunk, came up to my face, to the side of my face. I could smell tobacco, his voice was hoarse. He said, How many tons can you dig a day dago, oh dago, go dig.

Let Antenore fight. Good for him. So bold. *La terra è di chi la lavora,* he says. The land belongs to those who work it, he says. Lecturing everyone. Making speeches up through the bunk to me. *Vittime come noi,* he said. Victims like us have the right, the responsibility, to liberate ourselves, he said. Shouting. Enrico Orlandini rolled over in his bunk on the other side of the room and told him, Shut up, enough with the politics. Do you want us all carted away? Antenore shouted even more, This is not politics. Politics is the governor and the capitalists conspiring to bring in an army to put down the worker, to deny him the right to an eight-hour day, which the people of the state have already voted for in a just election. I said, Enough with the politics. Antenore jumped out of bed, stood up, and said, Politics is the luxury of those with power. Politics divides the workers. The liberation of the workers must begin with the workers. Unity.

I said to him I had heard about unity, about those salt miners in France who killed ninety-three of their Italian brothers. *Ecco l'unità tua,* I said. That is your unity.

Antenore was standing next to me, reaching up. He grabbed me by the collar. Go ahead, he said, hide yourself. That is who you are named for, Egidio, that hermit-saint, go bury yourself, see how the capitalists protect you. Go ahead and burn underground.

I say, let him go, let him be the hero; he'll end up with less than he has now.

There is no movement at all on the plain. Soon the animals will start to creep out from under scrub bushes and the rabbits will come out of their holes.

Shoreline

The tavern doors were closed, not propped open with a wooden wedge like on hot days, when you'd go by as fast as you could, not wanting to look in, but occasionally, you'd look out of curiosity into that darkened tap room, and the man sitting at the end of the bar, his head scrunched into his shoulders, a cigarette squeezed between thumb and index finger, would look up from his beer, rotate his head to the right, and give you a look of I don't know what, contempt, then look back down again into his glass.

We carried our books in satchels. We walked three abreast on the sidewalk. Rodie was in the middle. Wednesday afternoon was my day off at the grocery store. On Monday I priced, on Tuesday I shelved, on Thursday I cleaned the windows and dusted, on Friday I stocked the shelves some more and swept.

In that one short stretch on Railway Avenue were Parenti's and Castelli's and Lucenti's. The Parentis owned the Thin Dime, the Castellis owned the North Shore, and the Lucentis owned the Rainbow. Our fathers went to Parenti's after work and the Rainbow was for enlisted men. There were thirty-seven taverns in town. The war was over, but there were still soldiers stationed at the fort, waiting to be shipped out.

When we passed the Rainbow, the door swung open, and two soldiers walked out onto the sidewalk. One hooted. The other one said, Hey ladies, wanna take a sentimental journey?

Don't they know how old we are?

Sunta said this. She was indignant.

Of course they know how old we are, said Rodie. They're pathetic.

One of them had pimples.

What if they try to talk to us? Sunta said.

They'll slur their words, said Rodie, and won't make any sense.

Rina, she said to me, why don't you just start reciting that poem you recited in school, that'll scare them away. They'll figure you're some kind of kook and leave us all alone.

Sunta laughed.

Rodie put an arm through Sunta's and an arm through mine, and she walked a little faster. The sidewalk underneath our feet was buckled and uneven.

Go ahead, she said, and try it.

I looked up to the sky and said in a very loud, enunciating, voice, Keeping time, time, time. In a sort of runic rhyme.

Sunta and Rodie giggled silly, eighth-grade-girl laughs.

Go ahead, turn around and recite it, Rodie said. I dare you.

I double dare you, Sunta said.

No, I said, let's just keep walking and those enlisted creeps will go away.

My father says they're all just disappointed there's no more war, so they have to go around town acting like extra tough tough-guys, Rodie said. He says that all the hard work's done, and now all they have to do is go to Germany to pass out chocolate and stockings to frauleins in Berlin.

Yeah, I said. Yeah.

We passed Castelli's. Chief Pignarelli was coming out.

Good afternoon girls.

Hello Chief.

He passed by us and walked past the soldiers and said to them, Good afternoon Privates.

I looked back over my shoulder and he had fallen into line behind us, walking behind the two soldiers. He was whistling a song, it was from *L'italiana in Algeria.*

We turned left at Highwood Avenue and walked across the tracks. There was a train at a great distance coming from the south. We turned right at the next intersection, and the soldiers turned left, with Chief Pignarelli whistling behind them, following them back to the fort.

Do you think we should still go? Sunta asked.

Sure, said Rodie. I'm game.

Okay, I said.

At the intersection were two taverns, Pal Minorini's and Jimmy D's Tap. On the other two corners were Jacobson's Clothing Store and Flagler's Drug Store.

We were not to leave Highwood. No one told us this, but we knew it. Stay in town.

Do you wanna go look? Rodie said.

Yeah.

Yeah.

We passed by Amedei's Garage, and we walked fast because Amedei was a friend of my father and if he saw us walking around town, he would tell my father, and then my mother would know, and then that would be it.

Ma cos ad ghè da girar qui e là?

She'd start in. *D'andar a zonza? Non t'ad ghè nient altr' da far? Altroché girovago. Ti do qualcosa da far. Macché.* What do you think, you can just walk around, here and there, up and down? Don't you have anything to do? Never mind traipsing around. I'll give you something to do. Never mind the vagabonding.

But the garage door was pulled down, exhaust coming out of a rubber hose that fit through a round hole, and we passed by quickly and crossed the street.

※

I kept looking over my shoulder.

Are you afraid of your own shadow? Rodie said.

No, I'm afraid someone will see us.

So?

We don't belong here, we're not supposed to wander.

Maybe you're not supposed to wander, but I can go take a walk if I want to.

A carload of soldiers drove right past us. One of them shouted out the window. Hey! Rita Hayworth! Who are your friends?

At Bloom Street, there was a little woods, a little stand of trees. I had thought, when I was little, it was a forest where a hermit lived. We turned left, now out of town, and kept walking.

Do you think anyone saw us?

Do you think anyone knows?

Well, we're not doing anything wrong anyway, Rodie said.

We walked down Bloom Street, past St. John's Avenue, turned right on Temple Avenue. Then left. The trees were stripped of leaves. The sidewalks here were smooth.

Do you think anyone saw us leaving town?

No.

How could they? Everyone's at work.

There's always some busybody snooping.

All we're doing is taking a walk, all we're doing is sneaking a peek.

We stopped at a place on the sidewalk and looked across Sheridan Road. Our hands were in our pockets. We stared at the lake, and the wind wrapped itself around our knees in that narrow band of exposed flesh between the top of kneesock and hemline. We saw the lake in vertical bands, in the spaces between the mansions. In the winter you could see it best, when the trees were without cover. We saw it at a distance. The lawns were great vestibules not to be crossed. We looked at the houses and wondered about the people who lived there and how rich they were, but mainly we looked at the lake, which was grey.

Rodie had the cigarettes, a pack of L&Ms. She handed one cigarette to Sunta and one to me, so we each had one of our own.

Rodie held her mittens underneath her armpit. She swung the cover of the lighter open on its hinge. I thought of the word *gape*. She used her thumb to spin the tiny metallic striker wheel with its tiny spiky ridges, but there was just the vain clicking, she could not get it to flick.

It's low, she said.

She shook it. Her mittens fell to the ground.

A lady her mother cleaned house for had given her mother the lighter. Her mother kept it in a dresser drawer in the front room, and Rodie sometimes snuck and borrowed it. Her mother did not smoke and so she did not miss it. It was a shiny silver, smooth, with edges that were rounded. It had a monogram, NMA. It had belonged to Mr. Meizel, who had a business in downtown Chicago, and his company made small metal hooks that were needed in the war effort.

Rodie flicked her wrist hard, like she was shaking a thermometer down.

That should do it, she said.

Here, she said to Sunta.

There was a low flame. We hurried.

Sunta cupped her hand around the lighter, and Rodie lit hers first. And then I leaned my head in toward her, my back blocking the wind, and she lit mine. I took very small puffs. I liked the way the cigarette felt between my index and middle fingers, it made the heavy woolen gloves seem somehow less fumbly.

The cramping was intense. Onetwothree.

What did you say? asked Sunta.

Nothing.

No, you said something.

I did?

Yeah, you did, said Rodie.

I didn't.

You did.

And I admitted to them that I was counting, that this is what I did when my cramps got very bad: I held my breath and counted. The first count was always fast, but then I tried to slow it down.

Oh, they both said.

After I had said it, I realized that this was not something everyone else did, which is what I had assumed, and I realized that it was something peculiar to me and that they would always know this. And suddenly it seemed that we would get very far away from this spot, that it would not stay like this forever and they would always know this about me, the way I counted when I had menstrual cramps, and I was comforted knowing that forever, no matter what happened, they would know this little strange thing about me, but I was irritated, as well, that they should know this about me, just because of one little slipup, irritated you could reveal so much with just a little muttering.

You do what? Rodie said.

I count.

You count?

Yeah.

❧

Did you hear that Alfred Vignarelli got caught smoking in the bushes underneath the rectory window? Rodie said this. The smoke was rising up from the bushes and Monsignor Reardon was sitting in the study reading the paper and saw smoke coming up from the ground.

How stupid can you be? Sunta said.

I don't think it was stupidity. I don't think he cares.

※

We saw it through the trees, at a distance. We saw it in the spaces between those houses. The distance from the sidewalk to the doors of those houses was vast, a space we never crossed. We never thought, Someday. But we looked just the same. We did not know how high up we were because you could not know the height unless you could get near the lake and feel yourself small against the bluff. The lake was always out there, beyond. If you look at the map, our town was right next to the lake, but if you look closely you'd see that the mark is a hairbreadth away from the shore.

The lake, you could not touch it.

※

You could not live there without inhaling the wealth; to think of appropriating it was impossible. To want it was a waste of time.

You were born on the wrong side of the ravine. My father said this in dialect. He said it made its way in with the air when you breathed. *L'evnu dentro coll'aria.* He said this in disparagement.

We were the daughters of laborers who knew words like *flagstone* and *pachysandra*. He could see we had begun to take a certain pride in things that did not belong to us. That we had become silently boastful that we lived no farther inland, an appropriated smugness. We might not be able to see the lake, but we get the lake breeze.

※

The nuns warned us about the future: Stenography will ruin your penmanship, girls.

My penmanship was excellent; so was Rodie's, so was Sunta's.

In high school we would study typing, and bookkeeping, and stenography.

We were doing things to lighten ourselves up, already in eighth grade. We tweezed our eyebrows, we wore lipstick on the sly. We bobbed our hair, cut bangs across our foreheads. We did not want braids and buns; we prayed our mothers would cut off their immigrant hair. We tried to lessen our severity, but our eyes were dark and deeply set, our noses sharp and angular, our mouths were lines too thinly drawn.

As we smoked, we looked at the lake and we talked about the dance on Friday night at the Community Center. We talked about whether there would be boys from Oak Terrace Public School and whether our parents would let us go.

We talked about the record player and the music.

Rodie sang, You've got to ac-cen-tu-ate the pos-i-tive.

We did not swim in the lake; passes cost money.

We did not swim in the lake; our parents were afraid we would drown.

We did not swim in the lake; they were afraid we would contract polio. We would learn to swim in high school, when swimming became mandatory.

We did not swim in the lake because they were afraid we would break our necks, like Charlie Menotti who dove from the pier where the water was too shallow.

The lake was not for us.

They were afraid for us.

They did not want us arrested: *State attenti se no ti mettono in prigione.* They'll put you in prison. They'll take you away. They'll put you in jail for trespassing.

I tragressori saranno puniti. Trespassers will be prosecuted. Posted.

There were only a few signs, just a few here and there, nailed to trees in thick woods.

But signs were not necessary, we did not trespass, we only looked. We stood across the street and stared at the beautiful out-of-reach lake, Rodie and Sunta and me.

Sunday

 woke up in a laundry basket well padded with blankets and the first thing I thought was, I'm not supposed to be here yet. All around me, it was yellow, fuzzy and soft. The basket was yellow as well, and I could see in between the openings of the plastic weave. I had been sleeping on the backseat of the Chevrolet and they did not want to wake me. Quiet, quiet, shh. I was carried in the air, along the stone pathway, one of the handles held up in front, the other one held up in back. I was travelling feet first. The basket was uneven, my legs a little higher than my head. I swayed from side to side. My body was tightly bound; they had swaddled me in a receiving blanket in August and I was trying to work myself loose.

If your mother starts in about the dessert. My mother said this, I recognized her voice. *If instead of saying, Thank you, she says, We already have a dessert, you didn't need to waste the eggs and butter.* Quiet, quiet, my father said as they carried me, first through an aluminum storm door that squeaked open, then through a wooden door painted green with a small window and a white ruffled curtain trimmed with red stitching. The entryway smelled like the basement, comforting and damp, with concrete stairs going down to where the cans and jars were stored, to the furnace room and the room with the extra stove where my grandmother cooked when there was company. Here by the door, it smelled like the basement, but it also smelled like onions, garlic, parsley, all sauteed together. It smelled like two different kinds of meat roasting. Chicken and pork. Potatoes, both roasted and pureed, spinach cooked with cream cheese. It smelled like olives and peppers. It smelled like stewed tomatoes and broth. It was moist on my face, like vapor.

Then suddenly, it was up, up, the inside back stairs; they were steep and I was now at quite an angle. My mother was in front and I could see the skirt of her dress billowing, it was white stiff cotton with sea shells and sea horses. The wide belt was coral. I saw the back of her knees. She had a run in her left stocking. When I came out of her, my balled-up fist brushed against the inside of that knee. It was the first thing that I touched.

We paused in the middle of the kitchen but they did not set me down and I was swaying in the air, faces peering down at me.

Che faccia. A man with a shiny bald head and glasses at the end of his nose looked down at me. This was my grandfather.

L'è un angelo, veh. A woman who wore glasses and an apron with cherries all over it. This was my grandmother calling me an angel.

What a doll. This woman I did not recognize.

A man with a voice like my father's tickled me underneath my chin. Uncle Norm here, he said.

A man with a dry calloused hand that felt like flaking plaster gently cupped it around the top of my bald head.

The woman beside him brushed her knuckles against my cheek, her wedding band cool against my temple.

When they had all finished looking and cooing, I opened my eyes, and I could see my father lifting up a lid and looking down into a pot.

On four sides around me, draped with a white cloth, was tatted needlework. The cloth hung in undulations, it fell with finality to the edges, it was not flimsy and swayed only slightly. I could see through the netting that the table's feet had knobs that looked like claws. The legs were stained mahogany; they were curved like my mother's legs and a breeze from the enormous floor fan in the front room wrapped the tablecloth around them.

The men were in the front room smoking. My grandfather Antenore and the man with the rough hands were in armchairs across from one another, a standing ashtray between them. My father and my Uncle Norm were standing in the middle of the room, their voices lowered. The women were all squeezed into the kitchen, and I could hear my grandmother's shoes, they had thick rubber heels, clomp, clomp, clomp, all the way down the stairs, down into the basement.

Every so often, someone would lift up the tablecloth, which would brush against the bridge of my nose and my forehead. I would see a face briefly and then it would disappear.

Above, someone would ask

Dorme semper?

Sè

She's still sleeping?

Yes.

After the cloth dropped back down and fell into place, swaying ever so slightly in the breeze made by the fan, I'd open my eyes again.

❧

Through the tatting, I could see the bottom half of the buffet, its legs straight and ribbed. The door handles were disks, they looked like yellowed tortoise shell but were made out of hard plastic. The dining room table and buffet did not match and neither did the chairs. Some of the chairs had straight ribbed legs, some had legs that were curved. I liked looking around. The chair right next to me was from the kitchen; it had strange metal legs, no back legs only front legs that bent backward along the floor into a kind of kneeling position. The seat was red vinyl, stapled into place underneath, and I could see where a few of the staples had fallen out and the material was sagging.

❧

A tavola, my grandmother called from the kitchen.

The men in the front room did not budge. My mother, in high heels and nylon stockings and seashore skirt, began moving around the table.

Clatter, clatter, clatter.

One two three, she counted.

Clank, clank. Four. Five. Six seven. Eight nine ten.

She was picking up the empty soup bowls. The table had been formally set, everyone had seen it. Now the flowers and the soup bowls were coming off. Clank.

Is he coming? My mother asked this, calling out to the front room.

Who knows. My father's voice.

Who the hell knows. My Uncle Norm said this. His voice sounded like my father's.

Is he bringing her? My mother again.

He said he had some business down near Aurora, my father said.

On a Sunday? my mother said.

If we'd a tried half the stunts he does, Ma would of killed us.

It sounded like my father but it was Uncle Norm.

From the kitchen, my grandmother called out in a sweet, amused voice, *Ma lu lè fa come vôle.* That one there does what he wants.

And whose fault is that? I heard my mother mumble this under her breath in the dining room. I was the only one who heard her.

She held the empty soup bowls in a stack low in front of her. They were heavy, I could see how her wrists were stretched and extended. I could see the circle of the bottom bowl. Heavy white restaurant china with green letters. My mother's charm bracelet slid down on her hand and the charms were dangling in the air.

I saw the back of her turquoise high heels as she walked through the door into the kitchen. I heard a thunk as she set the bowls down on the metal kitchen table, and then a vibrating clatter.

※

Above, knees pulled in all around me. Dark suit pants and nylon stockings. I smelled someone's shoe polish. There were stripes made of diamonds on my grandfather's socks; the diamonds were black and the rest was maroon. It was hot under all those blankets in summer and finally I kicked myself free of the blanket and could move my legs. I was comfortable in my basket, well cushioned underneath by wall-to-wall carpet overlaid with a cast-off Oriental from a rich lady in Hubbard Woods.

Well, we'll just have to start without him. My grandmother said this in Italian and she sounded disappointed.

Thunk. On the center of the table. The antipasto plate.

Where did you get the olives, Ma? my father said.

Where did you find the peppers? The woman whom I did not recognize.

Find them! *Macché* find them. They're from the garden last year.

The mortadella is from Remo's? My mother asked this.

Macché Remo's. I wouldn't set foot in there if you paid me twenty dollars. They don't sweep enough. It comes from Lenzini's.

The metal chair was nearest the kitchen. My grandmother pushed it back, it slid easily across the carpet, and she stood up and took three steps into the kitchen. Then, the heavy metallic snap of the refrigerator handle being lifted up, the puckering sound of the rubber gasket as the door and the body separated. A plate sliding across a metal rack. One two three heavy steps across the kitchen floor back into the dining room. Thunk again above me, the table shimmying slightly. The other plate of antipasto in place, the one with the *coppa* and *prosciutto*. The chair slid back in underneath the table along with my grandmother's knees. Then it slid back out again, another quick trip to the kitchen.

Scordo il jello mold. I forgot the jello mold.

Jello mold le nè mica un cibo.

Jello mold is not food. My grandfather said this.

That shows what you know, my grandmother said from the kitchen. All my ladies in Ravinia and Hubbard Woods and Glencoe serve Jello mold at their dinner parties.

Jello is a mineral, like sulphur or bauxite, that they pull out of the ground.

She told him he didn't know as much as he thought he knew and she sat back down again. Then, one more time, the chair slid away from the table. Back into the kitchen for bread.

Up and down, my Uncle Norm said.

Ma stai ferma che te fai 'na burrasca.

Just sit down, you're creating a windstorm, my grandfather said. A *burrasca* is a squall.

In a timid little voice, the woman whose ring had brushed the side of my face asked in the dialect if someone was going to say grace.

My grandfather laughed.

Not here, but they say so many prayers over at Rina's house that they say enough for us too. He said this in dialect.

Right? He said this to my mother.

She was laughing but I could hear her voice catching in her throat and I knew her vocal chords were too tight. She tried her best, and said to him in dialect, *Ad ga ragiôn*. You're right, she said, which made everyone at the table laugh, her talking in dialect, she being so modern and so American, especially the man whose rough hand had been cupped around the top of my head.

As they ate the antipasto, I studied the underside of the table top.

I saw where the leaves of the table fit together. I saw the gaps between them. I saw the places where the pegs did not fit so well and where there was a slight warp to the board. Three leaves expanded the table.

The underside of the table was rough unfinished wood, not smooth mahogany like the legs. I looked up and saw writing. I could not read but I tried to puzzle out numbers and letters. 247. G o t t l i n g. The marks were made in a loose black script, written with a black wax pencil like the butcher uses. It could have been directions for shipping or maybe it was the name of the person who had owned the table before.

⚜

Every so often, my grandfather's knee would hit a leg of the table hard and the whole table would vibrate. My grandmother would scold, my father and uncle would laugh. My grandmother told my father to make sure everyone had wine. *I bicchieri*. The glasses, she would say. Fill them up.

My grandfather sat at the head of the table. Behind him, the windows were covered with sheers and there was a short radiator underneath the sill.

It's good to have my brother here, my grandfather said, toasting the man whose rough hand had cradled the top of my head. Welcome to America, Ulisse. Welcome, Paolina.

When they leave here, they're going to Des Moines and to Phoenix, Arizona, to see Paolina's nieces.

⚜

Beneath the hem of the tablecloth, I could see the bottom of the French doors between the dining room gaping open, pushed against the dining room walls. It was impossible to close them because of the thick wool carpet. The doors were stained mahogany, the tiny windows glistened.

The floor fan in the front room circulated the air, the fan's head too big for its very skinny neck. I watched the head of the fan pivoting, back and forth, back and forth, even though they all thought I couldn't focus on objects that far.

✻

All of a sudden, feet were moving all around the table, nylons and high heels. A clearing of plates, a removal of platters. An olive pit fell into my basket.

Oh here, Desolina, let me. The woman whose voice I did not know said this.

Oh, no, here, let me, my mother said.

Paolina, who had wanted to say grace, started to stand up and my mother told her in very polite Italian that she should just stay seated, that she after all was a guest.

In the kitchen, my mother asked if she should rinse or soak.

Just soak, my grandmother said.

I heard my grandmother's shoes clomping down the back stairs, her voice turning the corner at the bottom of the stairs and into the basement, where she was muttering that you have to tell these young girls everything.

✻

The men pushed away from the table, waiting.

My grandfather and his brother Ulisse spoke in dialect.

Ulisse said that McCarthy was a *mammalucco*.

McCarthy was no idiot, he was strong, my grandfather said, un-

118

crossing his ankles, revealing more of the black diamond patterns that ran up his maroon socks.

Better a McCarthy than a Mussolini.

Medesimo, my grandfather said. The same. It's just they stopped McCarthy in time.

At the other end of the table my father and my Uncle Norm were talking business, almost whispering.

So you think you're going to take it, Norm?

How can I not?

Dallas?

They say that's where the future is. Opportunity. We'd be moving around a lot but I'd start out in an executive position.

Christ, that's far.

How can I turn it down?

I can just see it now, someday, Norm Gimorri, president. My father said this.

Has a ring doesn't it?

Have you told Ma?

At the head of the table, my grandfather was laying out the beginning of the end of the history that led to the death knell for true trade unionism in the United States. At the top now, he said, you can't tell them apart from the stockbrokers, all speedboats and Cadillacs and vacation houses up in Wisconsin.

My grandmother poked her head back into the dining room and said, Roberto? She thought she heard his voice when she was down in the basement.

Ma, Bobby's not here. My father said this.

Orazio, my grandmother ordered my father, go call him up. Maybe he's still at his apartment.

My grandparents call my father Orazio. Everyone else calls him Ray.

Ma, my father said, either he's coming or he's not coming.

Oh, for Christsake Ray, just go try him. My Uncle Norm said this.

My father pushed his chair away from the table. I could hear him exhaling, exasperated.

All right.

My Orazio's the only one who listens, my grandmother said to Paolina. The other two are just like their father. Stubborn, heads of concrete.

The phone was hanging on the wall in the hallway between the dining room and the sun room at the bottom of the steps that go up to the second floor. Every time my father dialed, it made a scraping sound as the disc rolled around. It sounded like an emery board against a fingernail, only louder. The two and the three were short little arcs of sound. The nine was long and drawn out, a rubbing all the way around. After he dialed each number, the telephone made a little muffled ding.

He let it ring fifteen times on the other end, you could hear a tiny far-off sound through the receiver. My grandfather was talking to Ulisse about arbitration and a new kind of mortar that was easier to work with in the cold. My Uncle Norm wandered into the kitchen. My father hung up the telephone, clunk, and it hung heavy on its cradle. He called out, Nope. No answer.

❧

Coming from the kitchen, there was a sound like a pebble being dropped into water, a liquid plink, a little pucker, then the sound of a full rounded immersing and a swishing all around, a cascading over the rim of the ladle as it was submerged into broth. Then, when the ladle was lifted up, there was a sucking sound, a tapping as it clinked against the side of the pot. A slight click as the ladle hit against the bottom of the soup bowl, the start of a gentle pouring, slowly, slowly, because you don't want to rupture the tortellini as you pour them out into the bowl along with the broth. Another dipping. Another. Inside the bowl, there was a little pond, with its own movements, with lolling and lapping at the sides.

Here, carry it to the table, my grandmother said to my mother. Be careful, it's hot. Be careful you don't burn your fingers. Be careful of the baby.

Should we move her? my father asked.

No, no, my mother said. She's fine under the table, just push her under a little more, in case someone spills.

Above me, it was all a choreographed procession. Slowly, slowly, one by one, my mother and the lady who had called me a doll walked from the kitchen to the dining room. They padded across the carpet in their high heeled shoes, carrying one bowl at a time.

From the kitchen I could hear my grandmother mutter, *Ma con quelle scarpe stupide zoccoline alte alte cum s'portavano le signore di Venezia.* With those stupid shoes like the ladies in Venice used to wear at one time, shoes so tall they needed a walking stick. She was mumbling but my mother could hear her.

I could see that even with their spike heels they managed to stay steady on their feet, that they were not tottering, except every once in a while when an ankle would quiver as a heel sank deep into a carpet divot. They walked slowly as they carried each steaming bowl.

My grandfather wiped the condensation off the lenses of his

glasses with the tablecloth. Then he pulled the tablecloth up and bent his head down under the table. He waved his fingers in my face. *Beati quando dormono.*

They're blessed—when they sleep.

When he dropped the cloth back down, I opened up my eyes.

Formaio? Formaio? the voices above me said, as the grated cheese was passed around the table and sprinkled into soup bowls.

Finally, they were all sitting down and no one was talking. Even my grandmother's metal chair was still and all I could hear was a slurping and sipping that was slow and hushed.

Ah, my father said. Holy food.

My mother got on her knees, lifted up the tablecloth and said, Are you all right down here? Oh, you've come loose. Let's just swaddle you back up.

Let me see, let me see. She's such a good baby.

This is your Auntie Florence.

Their heads were under the table. They were pinching the edge of the tablecloth and holding it up, like the flap of a tent. The table-cloth was draped over their heads.

Doesn't this baby ever cry?

She's such a good baby, she sleeps all the time. But when she's awake, my God, she's alert.

They were balanced on their haunches. I could see their movements through my eyelids and feel their breath on my face. Aunt Florence smelled like perfume, talcum powder and honeysuckle. There was a hint of cigarette smoke when they talked, they both smoked on the sly. Aunt Florence kissed me on the forehead, she smelled good, her lips against my skin were a little creamy, greasy, chalky, all at the same time.

Oh look, she said, I've left a lipstick kiss. A Good Housekeeping Seal of Approval.

But really, how *is* she? my Aunt Florence asked.

She's good, she's fine, she's small, she was early that's the only thing. Everything is very good and she's just as healthy as she can be.

I could hear the slight brushing of their nylons underneath their skirts, thigh brushing thigh, knee against knee. They were both starting to teeter a little on their ankles, slightly losing their balance.

Rina, my Aunt Florence whispered, I wanted to tell you. Norm and I are expecting.

Oh that's marvelous. A cousin, a cousin for the baby.

They moved their heads out from underneath the table and I could see through the tablecloth that they were hugging each other. When the hug was finished, my mother rotated her foot on her ankle and said it was all pins and needles.

❧

I heard snatches of conversation.

Did he say when he was coming? someone whispered.

Did he say if he was bringing her?

He said he had some business.

On Sunday?

The track is open on Sunday.

❧

Norm, did you tell them? My Aunt Florence was whispering to my uncle.

No, for Christsake, I will. Don't have an ulcer.

※

The meat is delicious, Ma.

Desolina, how do you make these potatoes?

John L. Lewis. Now that was a union man. These others are no different from the capitalists, with their big fancy cars and jewelry and their girlfriends with mink coats.

Tomatoes from the garden.

You put too much salt in the lettuce. She always puts too much salt in the lettuce.

Pass me the bread, Ma, I want to sop up the juice.

※

I must have drifted off and slept awhile because when I woke up they were clearing the dessert plates.

The *zupp'inglese* was wonderful, how do you make it, Desolina? I'd love to have the recipe.

My grandfather and his brother Ulisse were each smoking a pipe, giving off a sweet tobacco aroma. My father and Uncle Norm lit up cigars.

My grandfather peered under the table at me and squeezed my big toe.

A napkin, stained with custard and Chianti and a smudge of cerise Revlon lipstick, fluttered down past me.

Someone above said, Oh to sleep like a baby.

Rustlings

ay's away downstate, it's Veterans' Day, and the kids are out of school. *Forty from Dempster to the Loop, thirty minutes from the Junction.* The kids are not awake. Outside the window, above the stockade fence, it's grey. The weather is already bad, too cold for them to play outside. November. It changed like it always does, on Halloween evening, while the kids were out trick-or-treating. Michael a hobo. Adele a skeleton. And even little Theresa dressed up as a little tiny witch.

Rina Gimorri is drinking coffee that has perked in a Corningware percolator on the stove-top, the stove-top is electric, and whenever she turns it off, she pushes the button twice. Off-off. Always. Just to be sure. And when she leaves the house for any period of time, she turns it off-on-off. Off-on-off. Her way of checking. It is not like a gas burner, where you can see it if the stove is still on; if an electric burner is on low, you can't necessarily tell. If she had had a choice in the matter, she would have ordered a gas stove, but she didn't, the houses were all built this way.

Off-off. Little rectangular buttons that are pushed down into the surface, a shallow indentation on top of each. It is almost impossible to keep the space between them clean, the grease and the grime and the splatters of soup and spaghetti sauce splop in between them, glug-dollop-plop, and the only way to get it really clean is to wait for it all to dry, to harden, and use a knife, a pointy steak knife, not a rounded butter knife, and scrape in between those little plastic buttons, scrape out the crusty residue, being very careful because the stove-top surface is stainless steel and very easily marred.

She woke up adding and subtracting. The mortgage, the car payment, the monthly tuition bill. In seven months, the car will be paid off. That will be one hundred and twenty dollars more a month. The coupons help. They save fifteen dollars a week. Fifteen times four is sixty. Times twelve is six hundred and eighty dollars a year.

Ray is going to be on the road for a few days yet. He has a customer in Centralia, and then he is going on down near St. Louis. He has this territory practically to himself; it is too far, he says, for the Chicago-based salesmen, and for some reason not many from St. Louis cross over into Illinois. He calls at night from a motel. Their conversations are brief: This is where I am, this is the number. How are the kids? Did you talk to my folks? Yeah, tell them I'm fine, the earthquake was no big deal. The coffee sloshed in my cup.

At the dinner table last night, she and the kids talked about today. Michael wanted to go to the Museum of Science and Industry, go down into the coal mine. Adele wanted to go to the Aquarium. They compromised on the Field Museum and now neither of them will be happy. They will sulk the whole way down. The baby will stay with her parents.

Rodie and Sunta think she's brave to be driving downtown with all the trouble there has been. Last spring. And the summer before last. It was hot.

She is going nowhere near it.

But still. Into the city, by yourself, with the kids?

It's not so hard. A straight shot down the Edens.

She leans against a corner drinking her cup of coffee, looking at the red Hills Brothers can on the counter across the way, staring at the wiseman with the turbaned head who is lifting up his offering.

She looks out the window above the kitchen sink. The roses underneath are mulched and covered in styrofoam cones; her father does not cover his with styrofoam cones, he piles on dirt and leaves and hopes for a good early snow before an ice storm hits.

She sits down at the kitchen table and faces the wall. She scans the front page, looks at the drawing of Joseph Parrish's "Nature Notes" and reads the caption: Canada geese bicker constantly. They cease only to fill their bills, when resting or feeding, while the leader, or one of his delegates, remains on watch for danger, and whether he wants it or not, he gets plenty of advice from the rest of the flock.

It is a day off from school and she does not want to listen to them fighting all day long. She does not want them sitting around all day watching television. They are going to the museum. And that's that.

She walks across to the other side of the kitchen to get out the map, opens the drawer in the corner next to the refrigerator. The fridge. The kids are always slanging up their words, and here, she has to say, she is in agreement with the nuns. Rina is always very quick to correct the kids, especially Michael, who is persistent, insistent, with his slang. Adele still listens and still responds. We don't have to worry about those problems yet; she's still a little girl. She's young for her age, she's not in a hurry to grow up, thank God, and we're certainly not going to push her. She still gets out her dolls sometimes, not very often, but occasionally she'll get them out and set them all up. Theresa, it's too soon to say.

Rina tries to comment not too often but often enough. She tries to back off when it seems like she has been nagging.

I was thinkin'.

He was sayin'.

She reminds him: Think*ing*. Say*ing*. Pronounce the *g*, Michael.

Phone and bike.

Some words you just have to give into.

But Michael, could you please say *refrigerator*?

Um, like, yeah.

Like, um, yeah.

Michael, would you please not pepper your language with these expressions. You are a very bright boy.

She does not agree with the old-school nuns about certain things; they do not need to be checking her children's fingernails. But, here, she is in complete agreement: children need to be attentive to their language. They need to not be sloppy and glib and flippant and slangy. What is left of slang years later? You sound archaic, you sound trite and anachronistic, you sound like discarded objects look, standing out in a thrift shop, a stocking with a seam up the back, a tie with a palm tree, words that pop out from your phrases and it dates you, it exposes you. One little phrase can do that. Ray's older brother, Norm. His younger brother, Bobby. Both good examples. Hey sport! Hey daddy-o!

She and Ray learned the language with such great difficulty.

A napple.

The consonant melded with the vowel of the next word.

Napple. Nipple. Nappie. Nap-time. Napple.

Quiet class.

But it was too late. She had already heard the singsong that started in the rear, the others chiming in. The teacher gently corrected her. She sat in the front row.

They say children learn a new language effortlessly, but it was not effortless, it was painful and embarrassing, the process of losing all trace of antiquity, of expunging words the poets used, archaic now even in the birth country, words their parents still used, *dì* instead of *giornata*, *ugei* instead of *uccelli*. Learning to say instead *day* and *bird*. Unlearning and relearning to pronounce the American words they had already picked up. Sangwich and Napple. They worked hard to unlearn what things were called, worked hard to learn what they should be called instead. Old Mrs. Benvenuti sweeping the space in front of her garage with the curling broom her son stole from the country club, calling the concrete space her *ara*, her threshing floor.

She and Ray learned to speak without an accent. They learned to say the *th* clearly. *Thursday. Thirsty.* Not *Tursday. Tirsty.*

But the old words are always there with them. Expressions of surprise. Incredulity. The expressions of exasperation:

Macché

Macché

Macché

There was not a mother in town who did not say this.

When kids were told to be home at five o'clock and they came back at six with an excuse about how no one had a watch or they thought she had said six o'clock, the mothers had all said it: *Macché.*

Meaning, don't give me any of that. In house after house, children would maneuver for a little, teensy bit of leeway on some disciplinary question, the mothers having none of it.

But Ma, the teacher didn't say we were going to have a test on it. *Macché.*

Ray and Rina and everyone they knew growing up learned to speak well. Cleared out the double negatives. Not, *He couldn't give him no good answer.*

This, Michael has not started to do, he is not slipping back a notch on this account. But the slangy-talk. She has to keep after him, otherwise, he'll be yeah-ing, and yupp-ing, and eatin' and playin' and sleepin' and all her hard work will be for naught.

Adele still listens, but Michael, well, Michael is a lot like Ray. He has such charm, he's so funny you almost forget to notice he hasn't listened to a word that you've said.

Cool.

Michael is one of those kids with energy, so much dare, a performer, a ham. He jumped from the roof of the house they used to rent, stretched out, shouting he was Superman. Adele came running in. Mommy Mommy Mommy Michael jumped. What?!! He was seven. What what what in God's name are you talking about? And she ran out the front door with the baby on her hip and there he was, face down in the grass, he wasn't moving, and she handed the baby to Adele, and she dropped to her knees. He was completely still. Michael Michael Michael. And she saw Beverly Rubenstein running out of her house, running across the street. Michael Michael. He was so very still. Adele was silent. The baby was silent. She did not dare touch him; you never move a patient with spinal cord injuries. The cars were whooshing by on Ridge Road. Her worry was always that the kids would play too close to the road, that they would cross without permission. Michael. Can you hear me? And Beverly Rubenstein saying, Should I call an ambulance? Should I call an ambulance? Michael, it's Mom. He turned his head toward her. He had blades of grass on his forehead and his expression was one of sublime satisfaction. He said, Kryptonite does not work. And he rolled onto his back and started laughing, but then he stopped because of the pain, he had broken his left wrist. Thank God the house was a ranch.

When they were in the emergency room, she saw Augie Gentillini. His mother had been up on a ladder painting the garage, talking to Lucrezia Brugioni down below, and had fallen off, and somehow she had avoided breaking any bones or getting a concussion. *These are a strong, strong people, you wonder what in the hell they are made of,* he had said. Sometimes they still run into Augie at a Friday fish fry or getting a hamburger at Beinlich's on Old Skokie, and there's a little joke they share: Mothers and sons dropping from the sky. Jesus Christ, what next?

Now Michael is bringing the slang of the times into their house. Psychedelic. Weirdo. Boss.

What was it Michael said the other day? *Far out.*

Yes, Michael, farther than the moon.

Vigilant as she is, she has her own slang; she cannot bring herself to say *the children*. It sounds too much like she is putting on airs, as if she is pretending to be one of the old moneyed families who live near the lake, up and down Sheridan Road, up and down Greenbay Road, with their big long driveways with their gated entrances. Whose children go away to school. Who, as children, were called *the children,* not *ragazzi* or *ragacci*. It is more genteel, yes, *children* is more refined. Kids are baby goats. The nuns are right about this, but this is one of the few dispensations she allows herself.

She has found the map she was looking for; she has finished her second cup of coffee. AAA. Ray keeps bringing maps home, the drawer is bulging with them, and she tries to keep it neat and organized, but it is such a narrow little drawer. He wants them kept in a handy place. Illinois. Wisconsin. Indiana. Iowa. Michigan. Minnesota. Kentucky. Missouri. Ray has all these states. It's a new company. And towns in all these states are building new hospitals, and all these new hospitals are going to need supplies.

She walks across to the top drawer next to the oven and pulls out a bag of peppermints. Brach's peppermints, little red-and-white striped throw pillows. They're in with the Baggies and Saran Wrap and the Reynolds tin foil. The kids won't touch them. Now, if it were chocolate Hershey's kisses, that would be a different story. There is still candy left from Halloween. Last year she ran out and this year she bought too much.

<hr />

She sits inside the car, inside the garage, the garage door down.

She turns on the ignition.

She wears her old car coat, her snow-shovelling coat, her taking-out-the-garbage coat, her grilling-hamburgers-in-the-middle-of-winter coat. This red wool coat is fifteen years old, she had bought it before she was married when she was working as a secretary down in Evanston.

She opens the driver's side window.

She turns off the ignition and pulls a pack of cigarettes from her car-coat pocket.

It is early. Sunrise was at 6:33; sunset will be at 4:35.

Upstairs, she still has to put the summer clothes away, the drawers are bulging with T-shirts and shorts. It's November. She should do this sometime soon, before it's spring again.

She smokes Newports. She doesn't consider herself a smoker. A pack can last a month. She will smoke a cigarette if they go out to dinner, if one of the other wives is smoking.

Desolina, Ray's mother, suspects. She brings the coat up close to her nose when she takes it from Rina, before she goes upstairs and throws all the coats on the bed. Coat closets are a modern invention. What do you think they invented beds for? Sniff-sniff. Like a cat. Very subtly she does it. But Rina sees. Two cigarettes after dinner Saturday night, true. But in a restaurant full of smokers, it doesn't take a blood-hound to detect cigarette smoke in wool. Desolina has a sensitive nose; a sensitive nose to go with the sensitive stomach. Every single woman in Highwood has some ailment. Some never go out of their houses. Some drink, starting with a shot of Jim Beam in the coffee each morning, or maybe a shot of Carlo Rossi red. Desolina suffers from motion sickness. Forty years in this country and she has not stepped into a car. She depends upon the train, the Chicago & North-western now that the North Shore Line is gone. Desolina takes the train, or else she walks. She talks and talks and talks of Italy but how will she ever go there without stepping foot in a car? She couldn't get to the airport; and once in Italy, how could she get back to her house? The trains do not go up into the mountains. If they did, they would never have had to leave in the first place because trains would have meant accessibility, and accessibility would have meant employment, and employment would have meant food and *soldi*. Money. *Soldi. Scudi.* All the old words for money. Rarely does anyone say *dollar. Diezh scudi.* Ten bucks. Desolina walks everywhere, legs like a hare. Takes the train and walks. And suffers from nausea. So sensitive to smells.

Thank God my Orazio, she still calls Ray *Orazio,* doesn't get sick in cars, Desolina says. She says this in Italian. In Modenese Apennine dialect, in Highwood-ese.

He's on the road so much. He could not make a living without driving.

And Ray is making a good living. On this trip, he's taken a company car and left this one at home. Usually he gets a company car for the road trips, but every so often when he doesn't, they have to juggle. They have only this one car to put in the two-car garage.

Rina presses the knob of the lighter into its cylindrical metal cave and waits. The garden tools are all hung up on nails on the sheetrock walls, rakes, and shovels and a spade, an edger, an electric trimmer; the kid's bicycles are still down on the ground. The clutter in the garage has a way of creeping inward.

Pop. The lighter is freed from its cave, unclicked.

She pulls it out, examines the coils of a tightly wound spiral at the lighter's end, yellow-orange, nice, and she presses it against the end of the cigarette which she holds between her lips, teeth not touching it. The paper and tobacco lightly *ssh,* a quick singe, and she inhales.

Newports. She loves the menthol. The cool ping of it. The drop in temperature all the way down her throat and into her lungs.

She loves this car. An Electra 225. The car is sea-green, the olive and cream upholstery is brocade. She loves this car, not for its luxury; she loves it because it works, because she can count on it to start in the winter and not stall out at the stop sign at the top of the hill. She loves it because there is not a speck of rust anywhere on the body. The windows are electric-operated, little switches that move the windows up and down. You kids be careful of your fingers. There is no gum-chewing in this car.

She glances at herself in the mirror, at the band that contains her eyes and the bridge of her nose. The circles are still there, they're not going anywhere anytime soon. Raccoon. Is this going to be another one of those long dark stretches?

She turned forty this year. Just like Mickey Mouse. Mickey's birthday was in September, hers was in July. Happy birthday Mickey. Growing up we called you Me-key Mouz, but now we know better.

She sets the cigarette into the ashtray and carefully unfolds the map. One side is Chicago city streets. One side is the suburbs.

It's a day off from school, she says to herself, and I'll be goddamned if I'm going to take the kids shopping on Veteran's Day.

Chicago Motor Club is stamped on the map. A photograph of that fantastic building there off Wacker Drive, with the murals inside, up high. Maybe she can take them there as well if they have time after the museum.

She inhales, sets the cigarette back into the chrome cradle and checks the map.

A straight shot down the Edens, and by the time they actually get going, there shouldn't be traffic. *Stuck in car jam.* Michael said that many moons ago. They were in the car driving down to Midway to pick up Ray one Friday night; he was flying back from Cincinnati. There was bumper-to-bumper traffic and Cicero Avenue was a sheet of ice. She's relieved Michael and Adele are older, there's been a lifting from the shoulders, but she misses hearing their language being formed. Hearing them use an adverb for the first time. *Quickly.* Their literalness. Their visualness. Michael comes up with the quick ones. He's quick. *È svelto,* as they say. And he comes by it honestly. Ray's parents, Desolina and Antenore, no slouches, both quick. Too quick. If you could look at them from a short distance, they would make you laugh with their banter and their quips. Come to dinner on Sunday afternoon, just don't be a member of the family, and they will have you wiping your eye with the corner of a napkin. And her mother, also very quick. And in more than one language. Her father, no, he's not one for witty remarks. He's very kind and humble. So Michael has the genes, the quick-tongue gene, the irony gene, the you-want-to-verbally-spar? gene. It's only a matter of time before James D. Watson identifies them on the Double Helix. Adele, on the other hand, could not tell a riddle to save her life. *Why did the chicken cross the road?* She would get lost trying to find a rhyme for *chicken*.

It's not so difficult. A straight shot down the Edens.

She'll drive past Touhy, down past Irving Park and Belmont, Armitage, all the way downtown, get off at any eastbound exit, through the Loop, to Lake Shore Drive and head south, down a little farther, and there they'll be. Exit on the left. Park the car.

Her lungs lose a little of the coolness, start to feel a little like dried-out leaves, curled at the edges. She inhales once more and crushes out the cigarette. The black stick-hands of the clock on the dash say seven o'clock, so she gets out of the car, walks through the garage into the family room, two quick steps up into the kitchen, down the hall and up the carpeted stairs to wake the kids for the trip downtown. At the landing, she takes the piece of candy from her coat pocket, unwraps the cellophane, crumples it, crinkles it, sticks it back into the pocket. Then she pops the peppermint into her mouth where it clinks against her teeth.

Straight Shot

inally, they are on their way.

They have rumbled over the planks of the wooden bridge, past the bushes on the left with dried-out scarlet tapered buds that look like a thousand cardinals waiting to take flight, they have passed the wall her grandfather built, passed her school, passed the Japanese pagoda house, and curved undernearth the viaduct, *viaduct* is a Latin word that means *the way through*. They have curved around and are making the drive along the fort, the fort clinging to her left shoulder as she looks out the window of the Electra 225 with sea-green brocade seats, and her brother is giving her noogies by reaching his hand over the baby's head, the baby who is sitting between them, and they are all strapped in with seat belts, nobody else she knows wears them, but her father insists on this, he is on the road every single week and comes home Friday night beat, and says to her mother, Hi-ya baby, and says to Michael, Come here and gimme a squeeze tiger, and says to her, You gotta hug for daddy pumpkin? and says to the baby: Theresa,

Theresa, Theresa, a million times cuter than the Mona Lisa. And they are all strapped into seat belts because her mother pulled it tight across the baby's hips before pulling out of the driveway, and she is supposed to keep one arm across Theresa, her right arm, and Michael is supposed to keep his left arm across Theresa, but instead now he is giving Adele noogies, which she tries to tell her mother, but her mother is saying, Shh-shh! quiet! I'm trying to listen to the radio, *WBBM NEWSTIME, NEWSRADIO 78!!* with the little zip up at the end, and she says, So help me, if I have to stop this car. And Michael does the noogies a little softer, just enough to bother her, and somehow as he does this, he makes Theresa laugh, Michael makes everyone laugh, but not her, she is the one getting the noogies, his knuckles razzing her scalp making a comment about dandruff, and Adele is trying to ignore him to see if she can see the lake, there's only a brief spot where you can get a glimpse, just after the tanks and the army trucks, after the little patch of golf course, and there it is, all pearly grey, a little stretch of lake and sky. And then the lake is past and there's the watchtower made of yellow common brick and the gated entrance with the two helmeted guards holding their guns upright, the butts resting on the ground. She hates the word *butt.* Whoosh-Boom, on the right, a train hurtles by, completely without warning. Another curve to the left, and there are jeeps and trucks for convoys, and here you are, *Welcome Highwood,* the sign says, and the first thing she sees when she gets into town is the dry cleaners where her grandmother works. Adele is named for her, she has scars on her forearms. Then the restaurants and taverns. And you turn right onto Highwood Avenue and drive over the tracks, bump-bump, past the little grocery store where her mother worked when she was a girl. You turn right and then you get to her grandparents' house on Euclid Avenue. Her grandfather is out in front putting up the storm windows. And as the car pulls into the gravel driveway, rumble-roll, she remembers her mother saying on the phone to her good friend Rodie, I swear to God, I could make that drive backward with my eyes closed in the dark.

         ✺

But now that they have dropped Theresa off with her grandparents, they are really on their way, going downtown to the Field Museum on Veterans' Day, on their day off from school. Now, after the drive to her grandparents they make practically every day, they are on Highway 41, and soon they will be on the Kennedy, and then it's just a straight shot into the city.

On 41, they drive by mountains of stones piled up along the highway, the gravel company Menoni & Mocogni. The names Menoni and Mocogni are Italian. Mahoney and Maloney are Irish. Fini is Italian. Feeney is not. She had always thought it was Joe Fini who sang with the high voice on the Lawrence Welk show, singing *Oh Danny Boy* and *My Wild Irish Rose*, songs to make you weepy, songs that make her other grandmother Desolina cry in the darkened room where they watch TV even though she is not Irish.

Now that Adele doesn't have to keep an arm across Theresa, she can sit in the front seat, which is better because there is always the possibility that she will get carsick. Her mother thinks she exaggerates, that it's all in her head, that she makes herself sick. Her grandmother Desolina gets carsick as well, and she has to walk everywhere or else she takes the train. Her mother thinks she just wants attention.

Cloudy and cold today with a chance of light snow or snow flurries. High in the midthirties with a low in the lower twenties. Her mother always has the radio on.

All of a sudden, orange balls are visible from the highway, suspended above ground, strung with cord, a hole drilled right through the center of each, separating the parked cars that face each other, front bumpers nearly touching. Interlocking Os are painted onto a tall slab sticking out of the ground, like an obelisk without a point. The slab is painted white, the interlocking Os painted hunter green. One O is higher than the other, which is lower to the right. It looks like the emblem at the gate of a country club. Or two laurel wreaths overlapping. Caesar wore a laurel crown and the shared area of two overlapping circles is called the intersection. Old Orchard is where rich ladies do their shopping. Adele has been there for special occasions. When her grandmother Adalgisa needed a new winter coat and they hadn't been able to find one anywhere else, not at Jacobson's, not at J.C. Penney's, they went to Old Orchard. In the plaza at the entrance, there is a fountain with pennies on the bottom. You have to dress up to go shopping there.

※

This year, they are starting to learn Latin, and when she knows Latin, she will know many other things, she will be able to understand many different words, not all, because English words come from many different languages, such as Greek, halcyon, for instance, but with Latin she will have a firm foundation that will serve her very well, her teacher said.

Amo. Amas. Amat. A mole. A Mass. A bathroom mat.

Except aloud it's different because the A is not flat.

Amat is like Mott's applesauce.

Adele, the teacher says, Pay Attention. In Latin, though, she does not need to say this because Adele's brain is like a little sponge, a round natural sponge like plasterers use to clean walls. *Silva* is a forest; her aunt's name is *Sylvia*. *Barbara* means barbarian. *Barbara* is the lady up the street who lives in a red brick ranch. Ranch is also a kind of salad dressing. House? Thousand Island? Ranch? Her grandparents call the bottled dressing *quella roba*, that stuff. *Quella robaccia lì*, that awful stuff.

Gale Sayers is out for the year.

Michael leans over the seat.

This, the bad news for Chicago Bears fans. Sayers was operated on at Illinois Masonic Hospital for a knee injury sustained Sunday at Wrigley Field. The Bears beat the San Francisco Forty-Niners in that game twenty-seven to nineteen.

Do you know what this means? Michael says. Do you know what this means?

Sayers is out for the season. Do you know what this means? he says again.

No one answers him.

It means the Bears are screwed.

Michael. Your mouth.

Michael slumps down into the backseat right behind her mother. He is in the corner leaning against the door.

Well it's your fault.

It's *my* fault they carried Gale Sayers off the field on a stretcher?

Her mother is looking in the rearview mirror, trying to get a good look at Michael. Don't lean against the door.

I had a chance to see him play and you wouldn't let me go.

Do you know, young man, how much those Bears tickets cost?

You weren't going to have to pay a cent. Uncle Bobby was going to take me.

Where do you think Uncle Bobby got those tickets?

I don't know. People are always giving him stuff. Cars and clothes and plane tickets.

Bobby has looks, her mother says to her father all the time. Looks like he could have been a movie star. I'll give Bobby that much.

Her mother adjusts the rearview mirror, tilts it slightly downward. Her mother's eyes and Michael's lock.

I'm sorry Michael, I'm just sorry.

Michael slumps, sinks into his winter jacket which is way up around his ears. The open zipper makes a V, his face is in the middle. He is looking out the window. Her brother is glowering.

Michael is the one who will do important things, and not because he is a boy, but because he is older. Whenever Adele gets there, he will already have done it. He's the one who knows the songs.

He said to her, His name doesn't have a *Y*. It's Jimi. And it's Hendrix with an *X*.

Oh.

She had made him a card last summer for his birthday saying she would go uptown with him and buy him a record, an IOU birthday card, *Redeemable for One Jimmy Hendricks Record*.

He will see and hear and experience everything first, and she will lag behind and everything she says will sound like afterthought.

On top of it, she's on the young side. She's heard her mother say it and it's true. The girls in her class seem much older. It's not only the bras and the periods, it's everything else too.

She wouldn't say that Michael knows everything.

Adele!

Adele!

Adele!

Are you sleeping?

Are you sleeping, are you sleeping, Brother John, Brother John?

Pay attention.

Stop meandering.

Get to the point.

A *meander*, she knows from geography, is a river that is a dead end. But the dead end is a lake and the lake is shaped like a sickle, called an *ox bow*, but it is a lake nevertheless.

None the less is written spaced apart.

Nevertheless is written all together.

Already is run together.

All right is two words.

All right, Michael. Jimi has no *Y*, but it's a present to you and you should be nice about it.

Yeah, you're right. Don't cry. We'll go uptown on Saturday. How do you say thanks in Latin?

Gratias.

Michael is not studying Latin, only her class. It is an experiment, they are in a Learning Laboratory. The Learning Laboratory is a regular classroom. In the morning, it's her homeroom and in the afternoon she studies math there. They say children are like sponges when it comes to learning new languages, and that's why they're starting now, to get a leg up.

Sponge is *spongia*. It is a feminine noun.

In Italian it is pronounced spoon-ya.

Her grandmother Adalgisa's cousin's brother Fausto Cortesi went to Sardinia when he was a young man and then he went to Florida where he dove into the Gulf of Mexico for sponges. He developed powerful lungs diving underwater and is now a very rich man in Tampa. At Sunday dinner, they talk about his car. *In gà una Cadillac grand acsè, che cumincia qua e finisce là.* It starts here and finishes over there.

A lot of good his strong lungs and Cadillac do him now, her grandfather Ettore who was putting up the storm windows said. He's got emphysema now.

⚜

She knows she will be good at Latin. The words slide into her brain. She remembers them in columns as she learns them.

laudo

laudas

laudat

laudamus

laudatis

laudant

Lauder means to praise.

She recognizes words. She does not know this language, she has never seen it, but it's partially already inside her, and it's easy to take in more new words and find places for them.

Many famous phrases are originally from Latin: *If you love me, save me.*

Her mother started to cry, out of the blue, when she was helping Adele study, and Adele said this in Latin.

Her mother rarely cries but she prowls around at night. Once when Adele got up to pee and stumbled toward the bathroom, she bumped into her mother coming down the narrow hall, and Adele was so frightened, she screamed.

Oh for God's sake, it's me.

As Adele sat half-asleep on the toilet seat and peed, the words came to mind, *Salve, mater!* Her mother wanders around at night, unable to sleep, and in the morning Adele sees milk scum in the bottom of a pot and a plate with nobby grape stems.

In Paris, French President DeGaulle reviewed a mile-long procession commemorating the fiftieth anniversary of the 1918 armistice that ended the First World War. The radio says this. *In Chicago, veterans have organized a ceremony for later this morning at the corner of State and Madison.* The radio says this at the Touhy overpass. Through the windshield, she sees the Cicero exit up ahead. Cicero was a great orator. She starts to worry about the report on mythology that is due in three weeks.

A storm killed her mortal husband, and the heartbroken goddess Alcyone, daughter of Aeolus, drowned herself in the sea.

The Cicero and Peterson exits are one and the same.

Punishing the suicide, the angry gods turned both Alcyone and her husband Ceyx into birds later known as halcyons, or kingfishers as we call them today. Yet the goddess's father took pity on the couple and decreed that during the halcyon's breeding season, the seven days before and the seven days after the shortest day of the year, the sea would always be perfectly calm and unruffled.

She always copies out information word for word before she paraphrases.

Thus, during the fourteen days, at about the time of the winter solstice, the halcyons could sit on their nests, which floated securely on the tranquil water, borne by currents across the world, hatching their eggs.

The week before her father left to go downstate, her parents were giving each other the silent treatment. She worries they will get divorced. She worries her father is going to hell: Goddammit Rina. He said this in the kitchen when she and Michael and Theresa were already upstairs in bed.

It started on a Tuesday night when they picked him up at the station. He was on the six forty-five. It was dark already. Her father got in the car, she could tell from the look on his face he was beat. As her mother scooted over to the passenger side, he opened the door and saw them in the backseat and said to her mother, You brought the kids? I thought you were going to leave them at home.

The baby didn't want to stay home, her mother said. Adele can watch her in the car. Michael said he wanted to stay at home, he has a lot of homework.

It's Mike if anyone who should be seeing this.

Then they didn't speak to each other.

It's so silent in the car, Adele thought, it's like going to confession. *Think now, everybody think, think about what you have done wrong.*

He drove past the water tower and said to her mother, So you're not going to say?

Let's not get into it, Ray.

He looked at her.

She said, How was your day?

They're sending me on the road next week.

For how long?

All week.

Where?

Downstate.

Oh.

What?

Nothing.

So you won't tell me who you're voting for?

Ray, don't start.

You better hope the right guy wins, dear.

A vote is kept in secret. It's one of our rights of democracy. Michael has been lecturing me about democracy.

Don't tell me you're voting for Humphrey.

I won't.

The goddamn Depression is over, Rina. The immigrants can't get it through their thick heads, *teste dure, teste di* concrete. We're a wealthy country now. It's time to start thinking like winners and not walk around always wearing the *coprimiserie*. The misery coat. Humphrey's nothing but a holdover from FDR. All of you from Euclid Avenue think he walked on water, but I don't remember that your dad got even one lousy make-work job out of it.

It's not a question of the *coprimiserie*, Ray. Not at all.

Ray?

What?

Let's not talk about it. Let's just go and get it over with.

There was no place to park on Spruce Street. A few cars were double-parked.

What a circus.

Go around the block, her mother said.

He drove past the house and turned right at the corner. He drove slowly up Willow and there was no spot there either.

Nixon's ahead in the latest Gallup poll forty-two to forty, her mother said.

In Adele's mind, she hears: Nixon Nixon he's our man. Humphrey belongs in the garbage can.

Her father turned onto Spruce again and pulled over to the side to wait for a parking spot to open up. He left the car running. The playing field was dark but the metal backstop and legs of the benches on the baselines glinted in the streetlights. Along the sidewalk, men were handing out sheets of paper. One wore a straw hat with a flattened top, a Pabst Blue Ribbon hat. These men are electioneering, she thought.

You're not going to say who you're voting for?

Maybe I haven't made up my mind yet.

You don't live in Highwood anymore.

What's that supposed to mean?

It means the economy shouldn't be frittered away on some hare-brained giveaway scheme.

Oh Ray. Let's not go down that road again.

I'm just saying, let's be realistic about which side your bread is buttered on.

Then they were quiet.

A car pulled out on the right side of the street. Her father worked the car in, forward alongside the car in front, reverse, forward, reverse, forward. It was a tight squeeze, but he nosed it in.

His jaw was tight.

He said, Why don't you just tell me, why won't you just say it?

Her mother was staring straight ahead through the windshield.

When they went to get out of the car, Theresa started to scream.

Oh for Christsake, her father said.

Her mother exhaled, and said, Adele you come with us and watch her. Hold her hand, don't let her run around inside.

There were lawn signs stuck into the ground, banners wrapped around the trees on the parkway. Flags leaning from flag holders at ten-degree angles. Across the street was the baseball field and beyond it were the train tracks.

They walked up to the door of a colonial house across from the baseball diamond. In the dark, people were filing into the house, they were streaming. Someone coming out of the house said, *A nice voter turnout, don't you think?* Her mother told Adele to sit on the stairs and watch her sister. They sat on the second stair from the bottom. Her sister's plump little body was nestled in between her legs, Adele had her arms around her. Theresa clung to her and for once did not budge. She was scared of all the people.

The stairs were covered in powder-blue pile carpet, up above was a chandelier, and Adele wondered if they were rich. It was like a party, but somber. Most of the people were silent. It had a sanctified kind of feeling, like incense drifting upward or holy water being sprinkled. To the right, through a big rectangular doorway, in the living room, tables and voting booths were all set up. Adults took turns standing in front of a folding table, bending their heads over to talk to one of the three ladies who sat on metal folding chairs and looked through metal boxes filled with index cards. Her mother and her father waited in line with the others. She had never seen her parents waiting silently in line. Then they each went into a booth and pulled a purple curtain closed behind them. They were short little curtains, like cafe curtains. She could see her parents from the waist down. Her mother crossed her ankles as she voted.

So you're seeing democracy in action?

She looked up. It was Mr. Martin from up the street. It took her a second to recognize him.

She said, I'm watching my sister.

149

Good girl, he said. He said this heartily, and then he went off to shake somebody's hand.

It was very strange, it was like something she had not yet seen, a silent filing in, a murmuring, with some adults gregarious, slapping backs and laughing, but most of them serious and severe, as if they were there to mourn.

At breakfast, her mother said to no one in particular, as she scraped a piece of burnt toast over the sink, Well, it looks like we have a new president.

Michael stop rubbing your eyes, you'll make yourself sick. Her mother says this as they pass Lawrence Avenue.

I'm making floating follies.

The car radio says, *The earthquake Saturday was felt in twenty-two states, its epicenter in southern Illinois near Centralia.* Her father is on the road down near Centralia, but her mother told her it was just a little rumble and that she should just stop the worrying.

Why does she always get to sit in the front? Michael says.

Because your sister gets carsick so easily.

Adele does not get to take her Latin book home with her but must leave it at school. On the cover, the letters are in a type called Trajan; it looks like chiseled stone. Trajan was a Roman emperor who built a Roman forum, Sister said. It was a huge commercial center, a huge market, where everything in the then-known world was bought and sold, wine and oils, pepper and spices. Picture it like LaSalle Street, she said, if any of you have seen LaSalle Street. Banks, the Board of

Trade. Picture the pit completely full, then imagine that inside a stone building with pillars was Trajan's Market.

What Adele pictured was the Church Bazaar, folding tables set up inside the gymnasium, making little alleyways, many walkways deep and wide, like a labyrinth, each table piled high with clothes and toys, Christmas ornaments and styrofoam snowmen, plates and bowls and saucers bought with trading stamps, electric blankets, worn-out leather wallets, tennis racquets, records, cookie jars, a portable hair dryer with a plastic hose and cap, couches and recliner chairs, a lamp shaped like a bowling pin, boxes and boxes of puzzles. Mountains and mountains of jewelry, pearls and rubies and sapphires and emer-alds and diamonds which were all fake, bicycles and tricycles and skateboards, and books. A rack of women's lingerie, nightgowns in pastel powder-puff colors, winter coats with fur-trimmed collars, ice skates, roller skates, globes, pot holders, dehumidifiers. At one booth, a phonograph for sale playing *Nel blu dipinto di blu, felice di stare là su*. A golf cart with a handle, hats with netted veils, hats with feathers, brimmed and unbrimmed hats, a big straw hat with orange and pink plastic pompon flowers and stitched cursive letters, *Bahamas*. Stocking caps and hedge clippers, a Mixmaster blender mounted on its own private platform with multi-sized milk-glass nesting bowls. Carpet sweepers and vacuums, a set of Jarts complete with rings and over-sized darts. A baseball game with magnetized runners running the bases who jitter and slide on the electrified field, TV sets, Jello molds and model airplane kits, bassinets and cribs, a map of Ireland's coun-ties showing the origin of names, Barbie dolls and Tammy dolls, the teeny Betsy McCall doll, the gigantic Chatty Cathy. Scuffed briefcases and artificial Christmas trees, football helmets, fondue sets and kimo-nos, a set of encyclopedias with the letter H missing. Coasters and a

Singer sewing machine, washboards and toasters, a clarinet, a guitar, an accordion. Playpens and lazy Susans, ladies' leather gloves that go up to the elbow, picnic baskets and ashtrays, matching end tables and credenzas, baseball mitts and tiny teaspoons from foreign cities, cuff links and highball glasses, clutch bags and pocketbooks, clip-on and screw-backed earrings, a big-drummed lawn roller, peacock feathers and stainless steel jiggers.

This is how she imagines Trajan's market, with everyone trying to buy the goods fast, before someone else can claim them.

⚜

Okay kids, I need your help now.

Her mother says this as they approach the Junction. The cars are merging from the other expressway, coming in from the airport. Cars on the right are trying to, quick, get to the left over into the express lanes, and cars on the left are trying to get over right, quick, so they can make the exit. They crisscross at high speed.

Michael slides over to the right and looks behind through the window.

Okay Mom, stay where you are.

Okay you can get over now if you want.

There is a semi-truck right on their tail, he is barreling and honking his horn for her to get over.

No, you can't go now, there's someone coming, Michael says. After the red car, after the red car. Go Mom. Go now.

No, it's too late, he says.

Her mother is just clinging to her lane, the traffic is moving so fast.

The semi blows its horn again.

Adele can see his headlights flashing in the sideview mirror.

Okay, after the station wagon, Michael says.

Go, Michael is saying.

I can't see him in the rearview mirror anymore, her mother says. Where is he? He's in my blind spot, isn't he?

Adele sees it pulls alongside her window, a massive slab of grey. He is passing on the right. Her mother does not look over, she looks straight ahead. The truck does not pull ahead of her and paces itself with her car.

Mom, the guy's giving you the finger, Michael says. Can I flip him off?

No! For Godsakes No! No, Michael, just ignore him.

Michael in the backseat exhales a heavy breath. Oh man.

⁂

Addison Street comes quickly, and at the exit ramp, one sign says *WGN Radio and TV,* and one says *Wrigley Field.*

Santo, Kessinger, Beckert and Banks, the infield third to first. This is what she heard all summer long.

And it's gone.

When the ball goes over the wall, it drops onto Waveland Avenue and when Jack Brickhouse says, *It's gone,* it is usually in a deflated tone of voice.

⁂

All the way down into the Loop, Adele worries about her homework, the Question and Answer Take-Home Sheet that is due on Fri-

153

day. She has finished most of it, but she wonders if this is such a great idea, going downtown to a museum. She worries she will not get it done.

You are encouraged to use a *dictionary,* an *encyclopedia,* or any other *reference books.* Please answer each question in *complete* sentences.

Who is Archimedes?

What is a prodigy?

What is the W.P.A.?

Who is Carl Sandburg?

Who is Charles DeGaulle?

What is *Inside the U.S.A.?*

What is infantile paralysis?

What is schizophrenia?

Who was Savonarola?

What is the Book of Job?

Who is Ring Lardner?

Who is Buddha?

Who is Mr. La Guardia?

What is Harvard?

Who is Ernie Pyle?

What is a labyrinth?

These are all terms from the book they are reading. They have been reading it for weeks and weeks, one chapter at a time, and she has finished it a long time ago already. She has to keep going back to reread a chapter every week. They are going slowly in order to accommodate the slower readers, she understands, she's not a speed reader either, but it seems to her that they could be trying a little harder. In the classroom, she sits in the middle, to the left, and she can see out the windows. The room is on the second story, sitting among the trees, and each window is made up of small square panes, a few on the bottom can be pushed open with a heavy metal handle that turns downward. The leaves on the trees are gone; they were all there when they started the book. The author has written many other books. He has travelled to many places, and when she thinks of all the places he has visited and written about, when she looked at the list, it was like flipping through the pages of an atlas quickly, with little dots popping out at you, strange names, and then they're gone, and it feels like the onset of dizziness, from behind the head, the shape and size of a cereal bowl cupped over the back of your skull, and it shoots out little tendrils, like jellyfish tentacles around the back of the head and over the top, not giving pain, but a blip of dizziness, and then it's over. But there is still a dull heaviness in the base of the head where the bowl was. When she saw the long list of books he had written, it seemed impossible some-one could be that smart, could know that much about so many places, and she thought, Where was his son the whole time? And either the boy went with him to all those places, Finland, Russia, Czechoslovakia, which made the bowl on the back of her head heat up again, kind of a warm dullness, like after a bee stings you, not immediately after, but after the sting and there is a warmth spreading, a feeling like what happens right before you faint, a little warmth at the back of the head the size of a cereal bowl, migrating up and around the skull, and the next thing you know, Boom, your forehead is pressed against the con-crete pavement of the sidewalk in front of church, tiny pebbles press-ing into your skin, and you're drooling. Or, the other option was that while his father, the author, travelled to all those places, the boy was stuck at home with his mother and didn't get to see any of them.

Adele's dad travels to places with exotic names, too, Peru, Cairo, but they are both within the state. Sometimes he goes to Cadiz, which is just over the state line. He usually gets home on Friday night and they order out for pizza and he says to her mom at the round table in the eat-in kitchen, I am so damned glad to be home, which seems like not the best way to say it, as she can tell from the look on her mother's face which seems at the same time pleased and scolding. She thinks of that little boy in their eat-in kitchen on a Friday night eating pizza with his mother, and his dad in a place like the real Cairo, and she feels the inside of her head fuzzy because of the emptiness, because his dad's not there.

You have a headache, don't you? Her mother often asks her father this when he comes home on Fridays.

No.

Yes you do.

It's fine.

No, you have that look.

That look is his eyebrows stretched up into his forehead like he's trying to give his eyes a good stretch, and if he puts his finger in the hollow of the temple, even though he tries to do it nonchalantly like he's just having a thought, and he rests his elbow on the table, Adele knows it's only a matter of time until he says, I'm going to go on up to bed. And then she thinks about the pain on the side of his head, a ton of bricks, only it is the size of the head of a small Phillips screwdriver, like one inside the TV repairman's metal box, his nickname is Blitz because he's so slow in showing up to fix it, and it just pushes and pushes and pushes, and she sits there thinking that this boy's dad was probably in a big hotel somewhere with his head hurting just like that, and that the boy and his mother were eating pizza all alone, and she felt very bad for that boy. As the teacher was explaining and explaining about the Question and Answer Sheet, she said that the author was once a correspondent for the *Chicago Daily News*. On top of everything, the mother and the father in the book are divorced, which Adele cannot reconcile. To have a son so sick, to have had him die, it seems like they would have clung to each other.

And when Adele found out that the author had gotten the title of his book from something else, she felt like he had cheated. Like he had shoplifted it from the candy shelf at Woolworth's. The title came from a poem. For extra credit, they can memorize it. Her mother is helping her and she will get the chance to recite it next week.

> Death, be not proud, though some have called thee
> Mighty and dreadful, for thou art not so:

She knew the poem by heart.

> Thou'rt slave to fate, chance, kings, and desperate men,
> And dost with poison, war, and sickness dwell;
> And poppy or charms can make us sleep as well
> And better than thy stroke. Why swell'st thou then?

What does this mean, class? Why, *Why swell'st thou then?*

It doesn't mean swelling up like a balloon, it means to get puffy with pride. What have you got to be so proud of Death? You think you're so great. But you're not. That's what this poem means.

Adele has never seen a real poppy. Poppies make you sleep, the teacher said, and red poppies represent consolation. They make opium from poppies, her brother Michael said.

Class, the teacher said. The poet's name is John Donne.

When she said this, she looked directly at Johnny Dunn, and he turned beet red.

Adele has to keep rereading the chapters, so they remain fresh in her mind.

The bump looked like two tomatoes. The bump had begun to exude large amounts of pus every day.

Sloughing itself slowly out of Johnny's head.

She thought that she recognized the word *slough*. Her grandfather Antenore uses it, pronounces it *slew*. Before there were golf courses, it was all slough around here. Swamps and marshes. And the slough had to be drained, like they drained the Maremma in Italy. Mosquitoes and malaria, down in the Maremma, which is where my uncle died. Before there were golf courses, there were Indian trails. Before that, there was a glacier which left moraines and cut out ravines and bluffs over by the lake. This is where they get the names like Ravinia. Lake Bluff. The Moraine Hotel.

Her grandfather Antenore knows many things, probably more than anyone, but she cannot forgive him because he deliberately scratched her grandmother's record, knocked the arm across the record and sent the needle skittering, then he said to her in English, Forget about goddamned Old World songs, they are nothing but nostalgia.

Every weekend, she rereads a chapter.

The tumor is in the right occipital parietal lobe. It is like a marble stuck in jelly.

If the surgeon goes too deep, the patient dies of loss of blood, or worse, so much healthy brain tissue has to be destroyed that he will be better dead.

Blood clot, tumor, X-ray therapy.

He was grey and seared as if drawn by Blake. Who is Blake? the teacher asks.

Was the tumor encapsulated? Answer in *complete* sentences.

No, the tumor was not encapsulated. It was the size of an orange.

The boy wore a huge turban of bandages on his head that was marked THIS SIDE UP. She thinks of the boy's turbaned head, pictures the wiseman raising his hands on the red Hills Brothers coffee can.

Brian Shaunessey can't stand the book and he makes no secret of this. He is the ideal. He is aloof and cynical, and also very insightful. He is unafraid. When the teacher steps out of the classroom, he beats the desk top with two pencils and he starts singing, *Oh Susie Q.*

Brian Shaunessey responded to one of the teacher's questions: It's like the author's always trying to make his son out to be some kind of genius.

Can you point out a place in the book that shows us this?

Yeah. Page 32.

Would you please read it aloud?

Yeah. *Johnny used to say, or perhaps it was Frances, that he resembled Buddha.* What kind of kid compares himself with Buddha?

Brian Shaunessey's parents are divorced and the teacher treats him like he is an expert on that subject.

The teacher read a paragraph that said, *We are closer I think than most busy fathers with growing sons.*

What do you think, Brian?

Brian Shaunessey said, That father is kidding himself.

At home, Adele reread that paragraph. First the author says how close he is to his son. Then he says Johnny spends the winter and spring holidays with him in New York, and the summers with Frances, the boy's mother, in Connecticut. Where was he the rest of the year? Oh. He went away to a boarding school. She kept thinking of him as being her age and had to keep reminding herself that he was much older, that he was in high school.

I heard them drilling those holes through my skull, also the sound of my brains sloshing around, Johnny said.

Drilling holes in the skull.

The bowl of the skull.

She sometimes thinks she is getting a headache. It is not in the right parietal lobe like Johnny's, but above the right eye. She thinks of the boy's shaven head.

She's so impressionable, her mother said on the phone.

Sometimes they call her Tallulah. Sometimes they call her Sarah or Gloria or Greta.

Adele, why are you holding your head like that?

There's a knot inside.

Adele, you don't have a brain tumor.

I know, but it hurts.

Okay Tallulah.

She starts to worry that any little pain is a tumor. There have only been two headaches. The last one was in early September. They were not wearing jackets yet, they were not yet reading *Death Be Not Proud*. It started on the playground, waiting for the bus after school.

First the bus took home the kids who lived on the east side of town, over near the lake. She was waiting for the bus to return, she was playing jacks when it hit. She sat down on the concrete steps that lead up to the convent. It was like the rounded end of a butter knife, heated and pressing in her temple. She was afraid she would throw up. She was afraid that Mark Trovatello, who rode her bus, would tell the whole class the next day.

The other time she was younger: Mickey Mouse stood inside her stomach, which was like a big cave. He wore the sorcerer's robe with the stars. The sleeves were too long for his arms. He wore his Merlin cap. He stood in his Mickey Mouse spotlight. He stood in front of a scale, the kind at a carnival where people test their strength by swinging a mallet and hitting a metal plate. This forced a disk to fly up a vertical pole and if the ball went high enough it rang a bell at the top. He swung a mallet, then rested, then he swung again. Sometimes the disc went up only a little bit, sometimes it went halfway. Whenever it climbed high enough, a bell went off in her head, and she wondered why Mickey Mouse was in her stomach, pounding away with a mallet.

On the bus, each time the bus shifted gears, she felt it in her stomach. Her stomach's juices sloshed inside, making a small wave that went back and forth and slapped against the walls. The window against her cheek was cool. She left her book bag on the seat.

At home, her mother gave her an adult Bayer aspirin and told her to go lie down. Her mother had meant the couch, but Adele went straight upstairs to bed. She took off her uniform skirt, left the box pleats crumpled down upon themselves in a circle. She left her blouse and her undershirt on. Her bedspread was a cotton quilted cover, white with lavender asters and pink sweetheart roses. She took the top edge of the bedspread and folded it over, then, she crumpled it into a ball. She placed the ball on the middle of the mattress, then craned her neck, bent it over and laid her temple on top of the cushioned knot. She lay in fetal position. The bile in her stomach sloshed from one side to the other and she thought of the word *lurch*. She felt like she was still on the bus and that inside her stomach was one of those miniature wave machines that sits on top of a desk, going up and down like a teeter-totter, the wave sloshing and crashing.

She fell asleep before dinner. When she woke up, it was morning.

The headache did not come back, but she was afraid it might. There was just a little jumble, which she tried to keep to herself because her mother thought she was intentionally letting her mind wander. At last year's teacher's conference, the teacher had said, She's a bright girl, but she gets very easily sidetracked.

She should not be sitting in this car on brocade seats. She should not be going to the Field Museum to look at gems and stuffed birds. She should be at home doing her Take-Home Sheet instead of sitting in the front seat of the Electra 225. If she did not get carsick, she could be doing her homework in the car.

When was this book written and published?

1949.

How old would Johnny be if he were still alive today?

He would be thirty-nine years old.

Johnny was born in 1929. That was the year of the Stock Market Crash, the year millionaires jumped from windows on Lake Shore

Drive. Antenore her grandfather said this, Millionaires jumping from the Board of Trade.

Please keep your answers short and to the point. Name the subjects that Johnny was studying.

Algebra

Logarithms

Trig

Analytical geometry

Binomial theorem

It is all ahead, waiting for her; she feels sick to her stomach. She cracks open the window. By the time she gets to that age, seventeen, they will have invented more mathematics. There will be more geography, more science, more astronomy and biology, more literature, there will be more and more history. She should have been born earlier because it is so hard to catch up.

How can you tell that this book was written during a generation different from yours? Write three things showing differences between your time and his.

1. They listened to gramophone records.

2. He used a soundscriber.

3. He calls his father *Pop*.

Her father calls his father *Pa*; her mother calls her father *babbo*. She calls her father *Dad*; up until last year she called him *Daddy*, and sometimes it still slips out. Uncle Bobby calls Antenore *Pop*. It irritates the crap out of me, her father says.

They lied to that boy. They lied to that boy in the book. All he wanted was to get back to school, and they would not tell him how sick he was.

At Diversey, the expressway turns inward toward downtown and she can see the skyline. Down below on the right, she can see the small backyards, one pressed up against another, divided by a cyclone fence. The backs of the buildings all have wooden porches, and the wooden stairs make zigzags down the side. On one porch, she sees a barbecue, a bike, an aqua couch, a set of Jarts.

If you think I'm going to let you go to the track with your uncle, you've got another thing coming.

Her mother and Michael are arguing again.

Betting is not illegal. It's a legal sport. They print the results in the newspaper.

I've had just about enough.

Her mother and Michael are arguing again and Adele would rather think about that book where that poor boy is dying.

Tony the barber. Tony the barber is Italian. Her teacher made a point of saying this, and she was not saying it for the benefit of the Murphys and the Reillys and the Dunns.

Tony is the barber who shaved off the boy's hair.

Tony is the barber and in all likelihood he was Italian, the teacher said.

The teacher looked around the room, one by one, at Neil Vanni and Donna Rabbatini and Marcia Lenzini and George Ruffalo and Jimmy Baruffi and her.

All of them have grandparents in Highwood. Their parents came up from Highwood and now they are regular American kids. Most of the Italian kids' parents came up from Highwood. Not all, but most.

The Trovatellos did not. No one knows where they came from. His mother is a platinum blond, her hair is always done up in a French twist, and she always wears high heels. The other kids' parents have known each other from the time they were this high, from the time their mothers were nursing babies or taking them along while they cleaned houses in Ravinia and Glencoe and Winnetka and Hubbard Woods. Their grandmothers took the North Shore Line together, took the train to work, and when Marcia Lenzini's mother sees Adele, she always asks, And how is your *nonna?* And Adele has to figure out which grandmother she is asking about, Adalgisa the grandmother she is named for who works at the dry cleaners, or Desolina, the grandmother who gets carsick who cleans houses. They're asking about one or the other, depending on which little town their families came from, San Michelepelago or Ardonlà. Michael is named for a town because when he was born her grandfather Ettore was sick in the hospital with pneumonia, but he didn't want the baby named for himself, too hard a name, and he wasn't planning on dying yet, besides, so her mother convinced her father to name him for the town, which was also her father's mother's brother's name. Keep everybody happy, her mother said, so that there will be no confusion.

⁂

Week after week, she watches the boy die.
The edge of bone next to the flap in the skull wound.
The bone appeared to be growing back.
You could cut a person's brain apart bit by bit, and there would be no pain.
Five minutes after I got there I knew Johnny was going to die.
She woke up one morning with the word *pro-tu-ber-ance* inside her brain, broken into its four syllables. She thought of him as a boy,

but really he was much older, nearly a man, a high school student. But she pictured him as a boy, she pictures him as Michael. One night in bed, she prayed for him, then realized he was dead.

⚜

When they get to the museum, they park far away, almost at the very end of the lot, way down in back of Soldier Field. The car faces south, looking down toward Gary and East Chicago; smokestacks in the distance are needles sticking up from the horizon. Plumes of smoke trail upward and form a cloud of ash. Glints of orange and red are like spittle in the sky.

Her mother locks the doors with the automatic electric lock on the inside front door, click-thunk, then shuts the door.

B-11. Help me to remember this, her mother tells them.

Bingo! Michael says.

Uncle Bobby, and I am 11. Adele mumbles this to herself.

The wind is coming off the lake.

Adele wears no hat, she has left it sitting on the front seat, and the wind enters the tunnel of her right eardrum. Her right cheek stings, straight pins pricking. A group of people up ahead clutch one another, tilting to the left, slanted away from the lake at an angle. She and Michael jostle each other, push against one another, trying to get the spot next to their mother that is protected from the wind. Her mother holds her own hat onto her head, and Adele nudges in close against her mother's coat, underneath the raised arm. Michael slides behind Adele and wiggles in sideways, edging Adele out. Adele steps right in front of Michael, which makes him stop walking, and in the open space she has created, she backs in next to her mother.

She accidentally bumps her mother in the hip and her mother stumbles.

Okay you two, that's enough. You're making me trip over my own two feet.

At the bottom of the steps of the Field Museum, a man in a grey wool overcoat is selling red poppies. He is her grandfathers' age. He is wearing a cap on his head like a butcher wears, except it's purple instead of white. It's the kind of hat that can be folded flat and carried like a pair of gloves. His ears are red and his nose is running. In one hand, he holds a bunch of poppies, which are made of cloth.

Buy a poppy? Help a veteran?

And poppy or charms can make us sleep as well And better than thy stroke.

The poem is in her brain.

A poppy to remember our veterans?

Her mother says, Oh yes, and she opens her purse and fishes around for loose change in the inner lining pocket.

I'd like three, she says. She puts the change into the coffee can the man is holding and takes the poppies from him. She hands one poppy to Michael and one to Adele. The wire is green and thin and pliable, the red flowers are made of a stiff material called crinoline. The center is a little purple fuzzy dot.

The three of them stand at the bottom of the steps.

Her mother takes the wire stem and threads it through the top buttonhole of her coat, then she loops the wire from the back and twists the bottom up toward the top.

I'm not going to wear this thing, Michael says. Besides, there's nowhere to put it.

His winter jacket has a zipper. There are no buttonholes.

Oh, here, just give it to me, her mother says, twisting the second poppy into place along with the first.

Adele unzips her jacket. The wind is a vertical blade. She fits the stem through the top buttonhole of her cardigan and leaves the jacket flapping open so the poppy will show.

A Slight Blow to the Cheek

he ceilings are enormously high, and when classes change, the metal lockers crash open and shut, and people talk. There is a great cacophony. This is one of our vocabulary words. Most of the words are not this hard.

Our floor is one big square with a classroom at each corner. There are two grades, fifth and sixth, with two classes of each. I am in fifth. The hallway is linoleum, with forest green and cream swirls.

In the spring, we are going to make our Confirmation. When the Cardinal comes, he is going to ask us questions in front of a whole church of people. If you can't answer them, he tells you you can't be confirmed in front of everyone. They are going to give us a booklet with questions and answers to memorize. Last year, when I was in fourth grade, I saw the fifth-grade girls in the class ahead quizzing each other. They crossed their legs and sat on the concrete wall that runs around the playground. They had to learn all the questions in a thick grey booklet. A thousand questions. But they haven't given us the booklets yet.

They passed out brand new religion books in the beginning of the year. Nobody else's name was even written on the label on the inside cover. They said they were made according to Vatican II. I think they look like coloring books. Jesus has a sweet face like a deer. He has almond-shaped eyes. So do the apostles and the fish in the nets. The book says, Charity. Justice. Community. Yes. But what about those questions?

※

Today, after lunch, the principal and teachers from the four class-rooms stood outside in the middle of the hall and conferred. They do this all the time. They can't make up their minds about what we're supposed to be doing. Afterward, Sister Mary Ugolina came in and said that anyone caught with an ice ball would be suspended. The boys bring sock balls to school; they are not allowed to soak them in water and freeze them overnight. An ice ball goes farther, but it could kill you if one hit you in the temple.

※

February is almost over and they still haven't given us those questions. Nobody has said anything about them. Maybe I'm being a worry wart again. Last year, in fourth grade, I was. Sister Mary Michael grabbed my upper arm. She marched me and my friend Paula into her office and she said, You girls worry too much. Why are you wor-rying so much? Paula was looking at the floor, and my cheeks were hot. I said I wasn't worrying. Everybody was staring at us through the window between the office and the classroom. She rapped the window with her gold ring and they looked back down at their papers. She said to us, Now, no more worrying! She started singing, Pack up your troubles in your old kit bag, and Smile! Smile! Smile! She told us to sing along. We did and we didn't even know that song.

⚓

Last night, when my mother went to pick up my father from the station I told her I wanted to stay home. I told her I would set the table and fold the towels if she let me stay home with Michael. I didn't think she was going to but she did. She took my baby sister Theresa with her. I carried the towels into the family room. I was kneeling in front of the television and dumped the towels onto the rug. I folded the towels in half from bottom to top. The left side over the middle, then the right side over that. Then I put them into the basket.

Tet offensive, the TV said. They kept showing different places. At the embassy, they took down our flag. The TV switched to another place called Khe Sanh and I thought of that song, Over hill, over dale, and those caissons go rolling along.

I was folding one of the salmon pink towels when they showed one Oriental man pointing a gun at the temple of another one. He's not going to shoot, he's just holding the gun there, I thought. And then, he shot him in less than one second. My stomach turned over. The man he shot was wearing a plaid shirt.

I heard the car pull into the garage. I turned the TV off because I didn't know if this was something I was supposed to be watching.

⚓

When Sister Mary Ugolina crosses her arms you can hear her habit scratch. Her jaw is always clenched. She keeps twisting and pulling her neck like a horse, like she was still wearing the veil with the white cardboard around her face. The nuns wear soft veils with their hair showing and it seems like she should be used to it by now.

Today, she announced that the girls still have to wear head coverings to First Friday Mass. Miss Metz said it was optional, so I did not bring my head covering to school this morning. In line waiting to go to Mass, Sister Mary Ugolina grabbed my shoulder and yanked me out of line. She asked me where my head covering was. I told her it was at home. She said, I am very disappointed in you. She handed me a piece of Kleenex with a bobby pin that had the rubber tip missing. I stuck it into my hair. I tried not to cry. I would have brought my head covering from home if she had said to but you can see that the girls in seventh and eighth grade don't have their heads covered.

Besides, if your head is supposed to be covered, how is a little square piece of tissue supposed to take care of it?

We have a new English teacher. Mrs. Sheehan. Sister Mary Ugolina is not teaching English anymore. Just religion. Someone said they took English away from her because she is so mean.

I was finally getting used to Sister Mary Ugolina and now they change it. My mother says not to complain, that nobody likes a *gnola*. I don't mean to complain but I feel like a knotted-up jump rope. You can usually get the knots out, but sometimes by the time you get it all straightened out, you just don't feel like twirling a rope anymore.

Mrs. Sheehan came in and said we were switching English books. She said she couldn't believe no one had taught us the parts of speech. Were we losing all the basics? My ears were hot, I was so embarrassed.

On the board, she wrote, *Senators meet.* Her handwriting is so neat but I know she's not perfect either. You can smell the smoke on her breath.

She drew a straight line beneath the sentence. Then she drew a perpendicular line between the subject and verb.

This is going to be a cinch, I thought.

Inside the grammar book, all the example sentences are underlined in red. It looks like the kind of prayer book they used to use where the words in red are called the rubric. Sentences are broken up and some look like stickmen with tilting arms and no heads.

·

My best friend Lucy is the kind of person who quietly raises her hand if she knows the answer. She doesn't wave it wildly. If she doesn't know the answer, she can just disappear and the teacher never calls on her. If I don't know the answer, the teacher zeros in on me.

Lucy can sit on the playground wall and read during recess. I could never do that. There are all those voices. Even though they're not calling me, they might. I keep picturing Lucy in her bedroom sitting on her bedspread engrossed in a book. And then I think of me just kind of walking around the room trying to get settled, doing things like making sure the knobs on the dresser drawers aren't loose.

If I am quiet and concentrating, I can hear the furnace come on. But this does not happen every time I go up into my bedroom to study. I keep expecting someone to come in. Usually no one does. My mother says no one is going to bother me but I have to leave the door open in case there's a fire. If my door is closed, my dad makes a joke: What are you doing in there, printing counterfeit money? They're just checking on me, I know, but do they have to know everything I'm doing? I don't think Lucy has this problem. I'm sure her parents don't barge in, and her grandparents live in New Mexico.

When you diagram sentences, you have to make sure you draw the lines long enough for the words to fit. Otherwise, you have to erase and it's hard to keep the page clean if it has smudges all over. When Mary Ellen Beckman and Margaret Moore turn in their homework, you can't even see where they've erased. They use Number Two pencils, too, but I must press harder when I write.

We were supposed to watch a TV special last night for social studies. My parents didn't want me to watch it but I told them I had to for school. My father said, I don't know why they are making you watch this kind of stuff. I started to say, Okay, then I won't watch it. But then I thought about what it would be like if I didn't, that I wouldn't be able to raise my hand when Miss Metz asked who had seen it.

While I was watching TV, my mother was doing the dishes, and my father was working in the basement. Once, my father came into the family room and said, Are you sure you have to watch this? I told him that I did. On TV, Walter Cronkite was talking about a trip he made to Vietnam. He said we did the best we could.

Today is Ash Wednesday, and in religion, Sister Mary Ugolina showed us a picture from the newspaper of a nun standing in front of the cathedral downtown. She was setting dried palms on fire. The ashes fell into a metal tray. The priests take ashes and put a dot on your forehead to remind you you're going to die.

It's almost spring, and we still don't have the questions for Confirmation. Maybe we don't have to learn them.

Every year on St. Patrick's Day, I want to wear something green but I never have anything the right color, which is either emerald or kelly green. Last year, I wore a green head band, and hoped my father wouldn't comment on it at breakfast. That he wouldn't say something like, You're not Irish, why are you wearing green? Everybody wears something green on St. Patrick's Day. Even the nuns wear a piece of jewelry or a little green ribbon on their wrists. My father didn't say anything about the headband but it didn't matter anyway, because it showed as the wrong color, because it was olive green.

Every year on St. Patrick's Day, we hear about Ireland. How they all came from Ireland and the South Side of Chicago. The potato famine, St. Patrick, and the snakes. We sing songs from mimeographed sheets. By now, I know the words and don't need a sheet. *Oh Danny Boy. When Irish Eyes Are Smiling.*

I thought Sister Mary Ugolina would say something today about Robert F. Kennedy running for president. That President Kennedy was Irish and that his brother is running. I expected her to say we should pray for him, but she didn't. In social studies, Miss Metz said he was marching in the St. Patrick's Day Parade in New York City. Then, she gave us a lesson on the primary system.

The headline this morning is in huge capital letters. Bigger than normal. It says, *LBJ: I won't run.* I have to think a second. LBJ is President Johnson.

Presidents change all the time. Every four years. Why is this headline so big?

Mrs. Sheehan is sick so Sister Mary Ugolina is teaching English again. She said to pray because Mrs. Sheehan is very ill. Mrs. Sheehan's voice is gravelly like Senator Dirksen's. I asked my mother one time, What is wrong with Senator Dirksen that he sounds like a frog? Is he sick? She said, Nothing, that's just the way his voice is.

Sister Mary Ugolina is skipping over the rest of the diagramming lessons so we will not get to complex and compound-complex sentences.

When we came back to class after lunch today, there were two big cardboard boxes on Sister Mary Ugolina's desk. She didn't say anything, she just started passing out the Confirmation booklets with the grey covers. She told us we needed to start on the questions this afternoon. She told us we would be confirmed in one month.

One month? We have to learn all this in a month?

She told us we should have started to study sooner.

We should have started sooner? How were we supposed to start sooner when they didn't give us the books?

We started at the beginning. What is Sin? What is Grace? How shall we know the things which we are to believe? We read the answers out loud, over and over. Then, she made us all stand up around the room and quizzed us. Nobody got it right. Even Mary Ellen Beckman and Margaret Moore had to sit down.

She told us a bishop is coming. Not the Cardinal. The Cardinal is too busy. Only a bishop. A bishop with the same name as one of the boys in my class.

Inside the booklet, there are not a thousand questions, but there are hundreds. If they had given us the questions last fall, we would have had plenty of time. How are the ones who always flunk supposed to learn it in time?

⚜

By the time I got home from school today my cheeks stung from the graupel. Graupel is what the weatherman called the sleet, hail and snow. It is almost May, so I didn't bring mittens or a hat to school.

While my mother was picking up my father at the train station, I saw on TV that college students had taken over two buildings and wrecked the president's office. They looked like ants crawling up a wall.

After dinner, my mother hemmed my Confirmation dress. She said she wasn't going to wait until the last minute, that she didn't want to be rushing around worrying about the dress because she had other things to worry about. While my mother hemmed my dress, I stood on a kitchen chair. I told her, I don't think it is fair. If they wanted

177

us to learn all those questions, they should have given them to us before.

My mother said, I don't know where this attitude is coming from. What attitude?

This attitude, she said.

I said again, They should have given us the questions before.

My mother hit my calf which meant I should turn. Her fingers tapped my leg. I barely turned my feet. About a minute on a clock. I pretended I was a Japanese lady in a kimono and wooden slippers.

The yardstick slapped against my calf. I turned again. One time, I don't turn enough. Hit, hit. The next time I turn too much. How were we supposed to start sooner when they had the questions? Miss Metz said we got them so late because the archdiocese couldn't decide whether or not we would use them this year.

When my legs accidentally touched the material, the pins in the hem pricked my skin. My mother couldn't talk to me because she had straight pins in her mouth. She kept pinning and unpinning, getting it perfect. After a few turns, she noticed my knee was bent. She said, Stand Straight, in two syllables: Hmm. Hmm. Why can't she say, Dear, would you please turn a little?

※

I have it narrowed down. It is either McCarthy or Bobby Kennedy and I am pretty sure it is Kennedy. He is a friend of Andy Williams. My father says he can't believe I am for a Kennedy. My father says, This country is not a kingdom. There's a reason we don't have kings and queens.

I have already been thinking about this for awhile, watching TV, reading the newspaper. Nixon's the One. Nixon's the one for war.

That's what I think. His daughters make me think of little white anklets that keep slipping off your heel into your shoe. I cannot say the other part of my argument, though. It would undermine it. Bobby Kennedy has a son my age. I know we would be happy together in Virginia with many children playing football.

It is only ten days before Confirmation and they are still making us memorize new things. We are far behind. I keep forgetting the things I already know.

It's right after dinner, and I am sitting at the kitchen table. My legs are wrapped around the legs of the chair. The back of the chair is flush against the table and I am facing my mother. She is rinsing the dishes and loading them into the dishwasher. She is wearing yellow Playtex gloves. The booklet is propped up on the window sill above the sink, leaning against the pane. It is held in place by the plastic kitchen timer and potato masher.

She asks me, What is Confirmation?

I say, Confirmation is a sacrament through which we receive the Holy Spirit.

She says, And? She says it as two syllables.

I can't remember, I say. I knew it before but I don't know it now.

She gives me the first words.

I finish the sentence, To make us strong and perfect Christians and soldiers of Christ.

I have already missed a bunch of questions.

She snaps off one of her yellow gloves. She gets wet fingerprints on my booklet and tells me to go back upstairs to study the questions.

She is put out with me.

Goddam it. I think it without the *n*. I am visualizing the Grand Coulee dam, so it is not a sin.

I picture GI Joe dolls with those frog feet that rotate on ball bearings so they can be amphibious. I picture soldiers in camouflage with leaves on their helmets, crouching down in a wet rice field. Then, I picture tall soldiers in tunics, with leggings and slippers that point downward. Crusaders. Which is the name of our school's team.

They told us the bishop will slap our face to put us in mind that we must be ready to suffer anything for our faith. My enthusiasm starts and stops. What if they want me to say to someone, Unless you convert, you will go to hell?

When I was little, they told us that if a baby hasn't been baptized and is about to die anyone can baptize it. You splash water on its face and say, I baptize thee. I wanted to rush up to a mother who was holding her dying baby and say, I can save your little baby.

I want my enthusiasm to be there, but instead, it feels like when Paula and I set up our fold-up cardboard doll houses last summer after we hadn't played all year. I knew I wasn't as enthusiastic as I acted.

From the top of the stairs, I hear my mother yell up to me, Don't be mad at me, pronouncing "me" as two syllables.

When I got home from school today, the only clean clothes I had to change into are ones that I hate. I'm not supposed to say *hate*. That I dislike. A pair of wool pants that are too tight. Navy blue and orange-red squares. They zip up the side. The top that goes with them is in the dirty laundry, so I'm wearing my uniform blouse.

I'm not ready to do my homework yet; I still have more questions. I don't want to go outside to play. There's nothing on TV. I pull out the blue box of graham crackers from the cabinet next to the dishwasher. One of the packages is already unwrapped and the tan waxed paper is torn. I lift the little package out, holding it between my index finger and thumb, careful not to break any more of the crackers than are already broken.

I carry the open package to the kitchen table and fold my right leg under me. I start looking through the mail. My hair keeps falling into my eyes. Boring. Junk. The *Lake View Review* has just come. I flip through, not reading, just glancing. I am doing it for something to do until I get in the mood to do homework. Until my brain clicks on. There are times when my brain is clicked on and times when it is clicked off. When it is clicked on, I can learn anything. The facts about the Spartans and Athenians. I can remember that as clear as anything. Corinth. Delphi. Thebes.

Now, though, my mind is clicked off. There are stories about weddings and tennis courts.

Then I see a picture of a soldier in a uniform. It says his name and that he has been killed in combat at Chu Lai. Chu Lai jumps out at me. It just leaps out like when my father is setting up the slide projector. There is a big square blur of light on the wall. The only other light in the room is a square column filled with dust particles blowing out of the projector, and suddenly the blur on the wall becomes something. The picture gets sucked into you. It pulls from the edges and slides to the middle. It can give you motion sickness if it goes back and forth from focused to unfocused too many times.

That's how it jumped out at me. Not so much his picture or his name. That is all on the perimeter. It jumped out at me because of the way it sounds. Chu Lai. Because of the sound. Chu. Chew. Having a mouthful of graham crackers I want to laugh but I don't.

Confirmation was supposed to be a big deal and it was like nothing. After they made us go through learning all the answers, the bishop didn't ask the questions. He didn't even mention them. All through Mass, I kept thinking, Is this the part where he asks? Maybe now. Then he called our sponsors and us all up to stand around the altar on the marble step. I was in the middle with my aunt. He started at one end and moved across the altar.

When the bishop got to me, he rested his hand on my left cheek while he said the prayer. His palm and fingers were soft like my grandmother's. His hand smelled like aftershave. You could taste it, the way you can taste it if you are in a pool swimming and someone near you wears perfume.

When the bishop slapped my cheek, I thought it would hurt, even though they told us it wouldn't. They said it was necessary, the way a baby is hit on the back after being born. It was even less than that.

Confirmation was supposed to be a big deal and it was like nothing. After they made us go through learning all the answers, the bishop didn't ask the questions. He didn't even mention them. All through Mass, I kept thinking, Is this the part where he asks? Maybe now. Then he called our sponsors and us all up to stand around the altar on the marble step. I was in the middle with my aunt. He started at one end and moved across the altar.

It is the last week of school and the only thing left to worry about is what to wear. We don't have to wear uniforms, and before I go to sleep, I try to decide whether to wear something I already wore on Monday. I wanted to wear the smocked dress my mother made me, but when I tried it on, the armholes cut into my skin.

It is almost summer and we keep the windows open at night. Even with the shades pulled down, the room isn't completely dark.

On my nightstand, there is a lamp with a little white, square marble base. The lamp has a pink shade with white frills at the top and bottom edges. Next to the lamp is a mustard yellow alarm clock–radio.

In the morning, the plastic knob of the alarm clicks on. There is no music. There is news and it does not sound like regular news. The voice says: California primary. Hotel kitchen. Arab man.

I run out of my bedroom. My nightgown is too tight and my knees catch on the material.

My father is standing at the bathroom sink in blue boxer shorts and his undershirt. He is almost through shaving and there are thin little lines of shaving cream on his face. I yell to him, and keep on running into the bedroom, looking for my mother to tell her. I'm in here, she says. In here. She is in the walk-in closet, in her nightgown, kneeling. I think, She knows already and is praying. But then I see that she is looking for something on the floor where her shoes are. I tell her, too. My parents put on their bathrobes and we go down to see it on television.

In the newspaper at the very, very end of the article, at the bottom of the page, it says: At first glance, Dr. Vasilius Bazilauskas, the attending physician, thought the senator was dead. However, realizing there was still life, he slapped the senator several times in the face, saying, Bob, Bob, Bob, as he did so.

At school, coming up the flight of stairs from the lockers, I see feet and legs above me under the middle bar of the railing. People are tromping and dropping their books. They are slamming their locker doors. People are talking but I can't really hear them. On the other side of the railing to my left, the stairwell is like a huge shaft of yellow. Goldenrod yellow. I can feel how high and deep it is under my cheekbones. For a minute, I feel woozy. Then, when I am on the landing, just about to go into my homeroom, I think, Why should we have school today? The world should just stop.

It is the end of the year and tomorrow summer starts.

Working the Clock

She smoked then. She sat on the hood of the car and watched them. He was hitting grounders, he was hitting fungoes. It was June. The light was perfect. The green could break your heart. The baby was asleep in the car, on the backseat.

He waved to her with his mitted hand, wore Bermuda shorts, a red tennis shirt with no emblem. This was pre-emblem. Before the Munsingwear penguin, the La Coste crocodile, the Polo polo player on his polo pony. He waved his hand wearing the mitt he had had forever. There at Sunset Park, lifetimes before they bought this house with its back facing the ravine. She started out on the other side of the ravine with the other immigrant kids.

She smoked Newports as she watched him hitting pop flies, the kids looking over at her every so often, watching her smoke, their dark eyes, drinking it all in. She loved the menthol. The cool ping of it.

❧

Call me if you need me. IDLEWOOD six. Nine nine five seven. Edith Rabinowitz next door. She knows that Edy and Mort are still awake watching the game. Everyone who is awake is watching the game. Edy will be leaping up from the couch, dancing around the room, clutching a pillow.

Why don't you come over and watch it with us? she said.

No, I think I'll just have a nice quiet evening. Michael got tickets and took Ray to the game.

Ray wanted to know, Are you sure you'll be okay?

Go, she said. Just go. Your son gets tickets for the playoffs and asks you to go, you go, you don't sit in the den with a morose wife listening to Marv Albert.

But I worry.

For God's sake Ray, don't be ridiculous, you think you'll have this opportunity again?

If I can just get them through high school, this is what she had always said. Well, they are well through high school, well beyond. They've all got good jobs. Now what can she use, what can she tell herself to get herself through the dark periods? Her mother used to call them *i brutti periodi*.

She prays at I.C. Which is where one of the guards also prays. Once, at 10:30 Mass at Immaculate Conception, she shook his hand at the Sign of Peace, and she said to him, You're a real lifesaver. He's one of those players who makes the buzzer shot from three-point range.

When the kids were little, Michael and Adele and Theresa, she lived in shorts in the summer. Long shorts that went to just above her knees. She regretted giving up pedal pushers but they had gone out of style.

Are those shorts painted on? her mother, Adalgisa, used to say. Because I never see you in anything else.

✻

Rina Gimorri does not use the remote, has never learned to use it, cannot see the point of it.

Ray, she said to him one time, why don't you get up and change the channel, you really could use the exercise.

✻

It's quite a house they live in.

They have done very well for themselves. He had a few big breaks he had to pass up because he couldn't go out on the road the times he had to take care of her, but still they have done very well for themselves.

Her mother-in-law Desolina says this. She says this in dialect.

Who knows what he could have done, if it weren't for her. My other son is a CEO, but his wife didn't have problems.

✻

The circles under her eyes are deep. She thinks they make each pupil look like a bull's-eye.

✻

Just go Ray. But let Michael drive. After the game, the maniacs will be hopping lanes on the Kennedy, weaving on the Edens, the revelers with their vanity plates will be flying. Be careful.

It's not New Year's Eve, you know, he said.

☆

The commercials are eternal. They stretch out longer and longer as the end of the game approaches. She wants to know how this will turn out.

Two minutes left in the game. Two minutes left in the game equals fifteen minutes of real time.

☆

Are you going to be alright alone?

What do you think? Do you think I'm not FINE?

She grew impatient, IMPATIENT, with all the questions.

What business is it of theirs?

☆

They had made an agreement, a contract. She will not harm herself without first calling someone.

I'm sorry. I'm sorry. I'm sorry. She said this very often.

☆

She watches the Bulls spread out on the floor, passing and dribbling, Jordan to Pippen to Harper to Rodman to Pippen, Kukoc, passing and faking a shot and dribbling and passing again.

Stretching time.

Bending time.

If he makes this shot, I'll call Edy Rabinowitz.

He misses the shot.

Her brain is bathed, washed over, by a liquid.

She thinks of the words *bagno maria*. Double-boiler.

Her brain is washed over by a liquid.

It's a barometric pressure drop.

If they win, I will call Edy Rabinowitz. IDLEWOOD six. Nine nine five seven.

They have trailed the entire game, unable to pull ahead. She has all that she needs beside her. The bowl of low-salt popcorn, the can of Sprite, the afghan, the phone, the pills.

Dribble dribble shoot. Miss and miss and miss.

If there were a reason. If I had a husband who treated me badly. If I had kids who didn't care. If we had real financial worries. If one of us had health problems. There's no reason. There's no reason. I am so fortunate. There is a forest in my backyard. What is wrong with me that I can't pick myself up? They've all had it with me.

She watches Jordan move low to the ground, pivoting and swinging his arms like a pendulum.

Ray played pepper with Michael, taught him how to field grounders. This way, that way, quick-quick-quick, stay down low on those bent knees, pivot and roll, reach and grab and stay in front of the ball, knock it down with your chest if you need to, stay on the balls of your feet, lunge left, quick-right, come up with the ball and throw it, quick-quick, good boy, Mike.

The Bulls are in the championship again this year; if they win, it will be five times.

A Pippen jam.

A fallaway over Dennis Rodman.

The pills are there in case they do not win. If they do not win, she will take this as a sign. If they do win, she will take this as a sign.

Nike shoes. Gatorade. Pickup trucks built Ford-tough. Come on, come on, enough. Play the game.

Jordan muscles the rebound and calls time.

They swoop over the Chicago skyline at night, the three landmarks, Hancock, Standard, Sears, three strands of flickering lights among streets lit up like so many thousands of neural pathways. There's Damen, there's Cermak, there's the Eisenhower Expressway.

※

After the huddle, the Bulls isolate their go-to-guy on Byron Russell and Jordan calmly works the clock. He goes up for a fifteen-footer.

A Michael Jordan jumper at the buzzer, the vein popping out on the right side of his skull.

※

The next morning, sitting at her kitchen table, which looks out toward the ravine where the ravens are nattering on and on, Rina Gimorri reads the newspaper with relief: We have a series folks.

The Minnie Minoso Cure

ll you have to do is shake his hand.

You don't have to say anything, or do anything.

He always comes the same time each year, a month before Opening Day. He still has a lot of commitments, he makes lots of guest appearances, but he never forgets to come.

I always enter through the front door, I let them know I'm here. In the lobby, my fellow travellers are slouched and sprawled and hunched in chairs looking at the television set suspended from the ceiling, up in the corner, smoking cigarettes. Marlboros. Kools. Every kind you can think of. They never seem to know about his visit, or care, or they would not be sitting there telling war stories and watching Wheel of Fortune. Normally, I stay as far away from that place as I can because hospitals will make you sick.

I tell the lady at the Information Desk: the voices are telling me to buy a pickax and go to the cemetery and break up headstones and then throw the pieces of stone through windshields of moving cars while standing on an overpass. It's not enough to tell her I am hearing voices. The voices alone aren't enough. The voices have to be telling you to do something. The voices are not really telling me to swing a pickax, they are just yammering away at me in Spanish. But if they send me up to see the young doctor and I say only, *The voices are yammering away at me,* he'll just ask me if I have been taking my meds. Well, yes and no. And he'll sit and talk with me for awhile, it used to be half an hour, now it's down to ten minutes, and ask me certain questions, then write me out my prescription. Usually that's enough. I'll take the medicine, just enough to quiet down those blabbermouths. *Berborreicos,* all of them. They chatter away at me, so I take these little pills until I quiet them down. *Calle la boca.* Shut your mouth: I have a nice little job and I don't want you ruining it for me. I'll be perfectly calm, doing a very good job, politely asking, Paper or Plastic? and the voices will try to distract me. They speak in muffled tones, *vamonos, vamonos.* Sometimes they start speaking when the sprayer mists the vegetables, sometimes after the cashier pulls down the microphone, asks the air for a price check, and stands there waiting for an answer. So at those times, I concentrate even harder. I tell them, *No, I'm staying right here,* and I think hard about where I'm going to put what. You have to make a good foundation to get a nice rectangular base; heavy boxes are best. Apples above potatoes, pears and bananas on top of apples, grapes on the very top. Raspberries are expensive and I always put them in a tiny paper bag and wrap them good and make sure they're secure on top and will not topple over. There are some who bag who don't give a damn, who will just throw a box of Tide on top of a crushable box of powdered doughnuts. Cashiers are the worst baggers. I've had my job for seventeen months and I don't want to lose it. So I concentrate on my work and I try to ignore those voices when they're buzzing in the air. Last July, they named me Employee of the Month, and my picture was framed in chrome on a stand at the front of the store right next to the picture of the manager. I got a fifty-dollar gift certificate which I used to buy cigarettes; I saved myself a pile of money.

When things are slow in the store, they send me outside to collect carts because the carts have a way of just walking off. I walk as far as Irving Park to the south and up north as far as Montrose. I can collect as many as ten carts some days going around the block. Last week, I found one in the middle of the playground at the park, right next to the swings, sinking into those wooden chips they put on the ground so the little kids don't crack open their skulls. A teenage kid was sitting inside the cart, a white kid with a backward baseball cap, and pants as wide and green as a giant bag of Purina dog food. He was dressed like a thug, and the others were dressed the same sloppy way, sitting on the orange plastic slide. They were all dressed like slobs; I like to dress well. Minnie has always been a sharp dresser. I said to them, very politely, Excuse me, but I need to bring this back to the store. And the one in the basket said, *Sí señor*, in a smart-aleck way and climbed out. I was surprised that he climbed out. Then the voices started up. And the white kid said, Did you say something, sicko? No. No. And I told those voices to shut up, now, because those kids have knives in their baggy clothes. Cut cut. And for once do you know they listened?

Thirty-five years away from Puerto Rico and they still haven't learned to speak English. I try to keep them quiet by humoring them, talking to them a little, but if you ignore them completely, they'll turn on you. So I throw them little tidbits, like sardines to the seals at the zoo, just toss a little morsel out into the air and I let them snatch it up.

I talk to them a little: *Of course. I see what you mean. Certainly.* All of this in Spanish. They speak the dialect of San Cristobal, my tiny mountain village smack-dab in the middle of the island; the Latin Kings run it now all the way from Chicago.

The volume of the voices determines how often I take my pills. I count the times they say, *Vamonos,* and when it gets to be more than sixty-five times an hour, it's time to start doing what the doctor says. This way, though, I can cut back the number of times I have spasms, which get in the way of my dancing. I do it all. Rumba. Samba. Tango. Tuesdays. Thursdays. Saturdays. At La Playa Dance and Music Club on Humboldt Park Boulevard. Minnie used to dance all night at the Casino Español when he was a rookie in New York City. The competitions are on Saturday, so I never take the medicine after twelve noon on Friday; I cannot risk a big twitch, *un calambre,* during a glide across the floor. But I'm always very good about taking it the first thing after waking up on Sunday. Sometimes it's not until late afternoon, but I do start taking it again.

The doctor, his name is Ramsey, said not to do this. Do not start and stop. But what does he know about dancing? Do you think anyone would be your partner if, during *Mambo En Blues,* your neck and shoulders started shaking? No, your torso is supposed to be still, calm, serene; it's only below the waist that you're supposed to move. Or if the medicine made me trip during the cha-cha-cha *Cayuco?* I said to the doctor, We'll compromise; I'll take half. No, he said, Mr. Cansos, you've got to take the medication as prescribed; it's dangerous to your health if you vary the dosage even a little.

He knows my voices?

You should hear his Spanish. And he thinks he can manage them better than me. No, I know all the tricks. I know when they're starting to get upset. I know how to humor them so they do not turn on me.

They could make me lose my job.

They could make me lose the room where I'm living.

They could get me thrown out of La Playa Dance and Music Club on Humboldt Park Boulevard by the old Swedish church, where the boulevard curves around a big statue of some big Army man that they put up a long time ago.

I've got it figured out, and, so long as I go in periodically for tune-ups, everything moves along smoothly.

Doc. I call him Doc. I say, What's up Doc? He humors me, and does not let on that he hears this joke again and again. And we humor him, not letting him know that we know that he knows that people say it all the time thinking they're being original.

I've never told him the voices speak only in Spanish. That would be a violation of our agreement and they would turn on me because they are afraid that someone will crack their code, and so I have to agree to protect them. I also know that no one can get rid of them, especially this Dr. Ramsey who admits he cannot dance. *The best I can do is tap my toes,* he said one time when I told him about my trophies. I do not tell him about the voices' language because if you try to get rid of them and fail, they'll only come back stronger. Like bamboo. Hack away at it and all you get is a denser thicket. I keep that piece of information to myself and it keeps them from acting up.

The voices do not like the place where I live and they nag me constantly about it. A room to myself at one of the Meres. I live in the Windermere, there's another one called the Grasmere and a third one, I don't remember its name, all right next to each other. Red brick buildings, built the same way, with their names chiseled in stone above the front doorway. They used to be elegant, the way buildings used to be, a mosaic design of little octagonal tiles in the front entryway. The mailboxes in the wall are made of brass, also very fancy. My name is on one of them. We call the buildings, The Mares, like night-mares. The voices get more vocal if I spend too much time in my room, so I try to accommodate them and limit my hours in my room to when I sleep.

Mostly, I try to keep everything in balance. I'm like a maestro conducting from my little box, trying to keep the loud ones quiet by granting them a solo now and then. I point the baton. I reassure them. *Non preocuparti.* I'll take care of everything. A little extra medicine here, a little less there. A few extra cigarettes. Menthol is best. The dancing. The careful placement of groceries into their bags. But in order to really control it, I need to see Minnie once a year.

Minnie was fast, he was strong. He opened it up for the others. Willie Miranda. Bobby Avila. Chico Carrasquel. Luis Aparicio. Sandy Amoros. Ruben Gomez, who was Puerto Rican, by the way. Camilo Pascual. Sandy Consuegra. And even if Minnie is Cuban, it doesn't matter to me, because before Minnie, any Latin ballplayer was light-skinned. Minnie had hands. Did you ever see him field a ball or grip the bat? But he kept getting hit by pitches. It was because of his stance, he crowded the plate, and after he got decked by Bob Grim, he was in the hospital for ten days. Minnie knows what it is to get hit hard in the head.

This year, in early March, I called from a public pay phone at Frank and Sons filling station, across the street from the grocery store. The phone is next to the cyclone fence, off to the side, and I could be sure no one would overhear me. Frank and Sons keep a Doberman tied up in back of the building during the day and I had to wait fifteen minutes until it stopped barking before I could make the call. I dropped in my quarter and dialed the number. I asked for Community Relations, and when the woman's voice answered, I asked when Minnie was scheduled to visit this year. The voice told me the date and the time. I was holding a receipt I had picked up on the floor of the grocery store, and I laid it flat against the little metal ledge underneath the phone. I wrote the information down and I thanked her.

My troubles started in 1961, the year the Sox traded him away. I was in the army, stationed at Fort Dix, eighteen years old, when the voices first decided to start jabbering away at me. I was an intelligent guy, they said. They were going to train me for intelligence work, I could speak both English and Spanish, but the voices got in the way, interrupting constantly, knocking around inside my head. They made Minnie move around a lot. In 1957, the White Sox traded him to the Indians. 1960 back to the Sox. 1961 to St. Louis. 1962, another skull fracture, chasing a Duke Snider line drive. Then to the Senators. Back in '64. Then he was released and became a representative for S & H Green Stamps. No one saves stamps like before, a few here and there in the checkout line. After eleven years away from the majors, Bill Veeck brought him back to the Sox. Those were hard years for Minnie. Saturnino Orestes Arrieta Armas Minoso has never needed to wear glasses, he is still the same weight he always was, and he's the only player in this century to have played in the major league for five decades.

I've lined up a few days off from work. I told the kid, the aide, working at The Mare that I was going to visit my cousin in Milwaukee for a few days. Can you give me a phone number? he asked. No, my cousin doesn't have a phone, but don't worry, I'll be back. You have to reassure these college graduates about everything; they're so earnest and concerned.

Before Minnie's visit, I walked down Broadway to Wilson and caught the bus west to Damen and waited for a Damen bus south. I had my toothbrush in the left inside pocket of my suit coat, black with silver flecks, my starched yellow shirt, and my lime green comb in the inside right pocket. My shoes were shined and tied with brand new laces. It was warm and and I carried my coat over my arm. I took that bus all the way down Damen. It took an hour with all the road work. I passed the park where I collect carts, I passed the palm reader on the second story of the rounded triangle-of-a-building with her neon sign that says TAROT. I passed all the expensive restaurants in Bucktown with the names that are constantly changing. One afternoon after I got my disability check, I blew a wad at a restaurant called Le Couchon. I ordered a steak with fried potatoes cut very, very thin, and drank a glass of expensive red wine. The place is called something else now. Down Damen, past hubcap shops and *lavandarias,* Old Style signs that say *zimny piwo* and *cerveza fria,* past the Latin grocery stores, the old funeral home for the old Polish people, and when I reached all the broken-down churches with the boarded-up stained-glass windows, churches with long, long names, Bethany Mt. Zion Gethsemane, I know we're getting close. We crossed over the Eisenhower Expressway, where no car was moving, and then went past Cook County Hospital.

Then we pulled up at the front door of the Veterans Administration Hospital. I stepped down the stairs of the bus, went through the revolving door, and I walked through the lobby straight to the information desk and told them about the pickax. The lady hit the panic button underneath the desk with her knee and someone from security, this time it was Mr. Buford, walked me upstairs to five, and I told a different doctor about the voices telling me to *do* something. Voices alone aren't enough. It has to be something dramatic or they will not let you stay.

And now today, I'm all settled in, in for observation, and tomorrow afternoon, he's going to walk through the wards, visiting all the patients, giving out autographs, and I'll be ready when he comes into my room. I'll be standing up, sharply dressed, teeth brushed, hair combed, and I'll shake his hand and he'll clasp my forearm. He'll say, *Como estas hombre?* and then I will be approximately healed for another year.

With These New Tunes

aiku baby.
Wudja?
Wanna?
Maybelatah.
Baby you I coo ya.

But it's not a haiku, I said. Five seven five.
I'm a beat man, you said.
Drum roll. Ta-dum. Ta-dum.

It's so stupid, but you know my heart is tick-tock-ticking, thunking against the sternum.
Ta-dum. Ta-dum.
A song on the radio on a station I never listen to.

I was driving, sitting, and a song brought me to my knees.

Now? after all this time?

There have been others, scores of others, in that cerulean zone.

Last night was the first really hot summer night; you could see beads of moisture hanging in the air. In the middle porch of a three-decker that faces the park, a woman stood on the balcony tousling her hair, fanning it from behind. Odd, I thought, how exhibitionist, to be performing her toilette on a balcony overlooking the park; who was she showing off for? She was young, in her early twenties. A trigger-hair second later, I realized she was holding a dryer. And then she began to blow her hair dry. It was Saturday night. She did this with such ease, as if she were completely unaware that she was standing in public view, knowing only that it was too hot inside to be blow-drying hair and that this was the best place to do it, at least there was a breeze. She was not thinking of who might notice her from below, but thinking ahead of the evening that was yet to come.

It made my lungs contract and collapse, like an emptied bellow, and I suddenly felt old. No. I felt not young.

From a distance, I've followed your meandering trajectory. They've used one of your songs in the sound track of an off-beat major motion picture.

And whenever I hear of you, I start to feel again like clean crew socks just out of the dryer, too comfortable and new. What were you doing with me, even for a brief period of time? You knew it, I knew it, I was no bohemian, I was no hippie. If I had been a howler, it would have made some sense. If you had discovered that I had a secret addiction to heroin. Him? With her? That was what their looks said at all those parties that started at midnight. But no, when I think of it now, I smelled like shampoo, like aloe, which you, to my astonishment, inhaled.

⁂

April seeped in through the seams of the canvas tent, it was Italian-made, surplus supply cast-off from the Italian army, sold in the Army-Navy store. It leaked, not a leak of biblical proportions, but a trickle, and the floor was wet, and the sleeping bags we had laid on the floor were wet, and the blankets on top of us were damp, and it was cold, it was Minnesota in April, of course it was cold, but it was private, out there in an open field, where a little tent city had sprung up the night before. In the interval between night and morning, with all its little wakenings, it was damp and cold, and it did not matter, because when I woke all I cared about was you, I mean each and every impulse, ten fingertips pressed against your scalp, knowing that on the left side of the back of your head, midway up, to the left of the cortex, there was a bump. I did not care about the damp, I did not care about the cold, I do not think I noticed. When I woke, above I saw a thousand beads of water hugging the taut canvas, condensation and melt, and I reached for you underneath the damp wool blanket.

> We woke in an embrace.
> There was frost on the lawn and vapor rose up from it.
> The birds yawned and chattered sleepily.
> The dawn how soon it comes.

203

My God, who could do that now? Who could sustain that, sleeping always intertwined, wrapped so tight that neither can let go. Well, I know that I could not. Your backbone, the round corners of your angular shoulders; you said into my ear, I could feel your lips on cartilage, the reverberations in the tympanum: This is how it should be. Yes. Forever and ever and ever. I thought it, I did not say it. I tiptoed around the jinx, the hex. I knew enough to not utter it. I knew that you would wander. I knew better than to say it; who believed in forever? I didn't. I did. Maybe you did for that interval of time between the outer limits of a chord while there were vibrations still contained within it.

⁂

This morning, I completely took out the left side of the van as I backed out of the garage. A huge long gash, the metal bent crisply into a valley. The insurance premium is going to go up now. See? It would not have worked. The other day, I left the house with mismatched shoes. They were very nearly identical, one black, one brown, the same style of sturdy rubber-soled walking shoe. But still, they did not match.

You were going to wander. *Vagabonder.*

At a physical level, I knew that I could not. It was like a pit in the stomach, a hardened oversized chokeberry in my throat, and I knew I was not going to make any long journeys with you.

I had one chance. And my one chance was not to be waiting for you to come home from some club in Minneapolis, or Santa Monica, or New York City. I could see into the future, that was my dilemma. One of my so-called hang-ups. I knew the future. And so I could not make myself be light and easy. When I looked into the future, I did not see myself there as your woman, your girl, your lady, waiting in an apartment with a porch overlooking the park, smoking cigarettes in the dark. If I could have remained inside that chord, what would have happened? But I did not stay within it, because what I saw outside the diapason, outside that perfectly imagined chord, was whiskey and cigarettes stubbed out in saucers, half-filled cups of beer, a lingering haze of pot. I saw you sitting in a dining room, on a sofa with the stuffing coming out of the arms, playing your guitar, writing down words and notes in a little spiral notebook. I did not reject this part of my envisioning. You were smooth and long and perfect. Your eyes translucent. But mainly, when I looked ahead, what I saw was a kitchen table at dawn, in the back room of an apartment, and me looking through the want-ads.

Eram combat sobre-volers,
E sobr'amars e loncs dezirs

Now over-wanting assails me
And over-longing and long desire;
And overboldness and folly and unseemliness
make me pursue that which befits not my worth.
And if I want too much, in my folly,
my sense appears somewhat paltry,
but I remain noble and true.

This is what I do. I teach this. One semester every other year I get to teach what I want. Troubadour poetry. The rest of the time it's grammar.

Je suis un rock-star.

One semester every other year.
Sobre-volers and sobr'amors e lonc dezirs.
Over-longing and long desire.
The poem is by Giraut de Borneil.

Later in the morning, after I had taken out the side of the van, I heard your song on the radio. I don't listen to the rock'n'roll station much anymore, ten drippy songs for every one with something. But I had it on because they were fundraising again on the classical station. I was driving to the municipal dump, taking brown bags filled with dead branches and grass clippings, and when I heard the music, my tire bumped the side of the curb.

I wanted to be your one and only, but you, even then, needed more than one woman surrounding you. Even now, there are several. They have good hair, long legs, lips that can pout and let through song that sounds like angels; it's true, their voices do stir.

The dawn how soon it comes.
A man in bed with a woman who is not his wife, nor is he her husband. This is one of the stories in the poems that I get to teach one semester every other year.

I hardly know how to begin a poem which I want to make light and easy.
Un vers que volh far leuger.
Light and easy.

A foolish thing was my presumption.
Folors
Fo ma sospeissos

The folly returns every so often. In the latest version, I am on the verge of running off with a poet from Galicia because he speaks a language no one else does and he asks me to marry him.

My fantasies are so domestic, but you knew that then, and that is why you pulled away; I would have pulled away too, but I was stuck with myself.

Your fantasies always end with marriage, you said.

How could you have known that? I didn't say that. I denied it.

I was inhaling a Marlboro. I was drinking a Grain Belt beer. Jerry Garcia was on the juke box singing *Stella Blue*. It was snowing outside. And I felt a stab in the depths of my left temple. Migraine. And I said to you, What do you know about my fantasies? I stood up and nearly passed out from the nausea that was just beginning. I walked past the other tables into the barroom, and I ordered a shot from Jim the bartender and I drank it. My head grew larger and the throbbing got stronger. I said some good nights, then I walked out the door. I remember the ice squeaking beneath my feet at such a high pitch that it caused a knock inside my head each time I stepped.

I walked back to campus, and I could hardly see. It was snowing but that was not the problem, it was my eyes. I heard footsteps behind me, and it was you, and you had brought me my jacket.

We went to bed. We slept.

You said that you were sorry.

So you've escaped, haven't you? Forty-two years old and you've escaped. Found all those escape clauses.

One of my closest friends then said to me, as I sat on the edge of the bed at midterm, He's never going to marry you.

It hadn't crossed my mind to marry you, or anyone else, I was twenty years old, that state of being was so far away, a maybe that had nothing to do with me. Who was thinking of marriage? It was not what I was angling for, fishing for, and this was what she implied in her voice, that I was trying to snag you.

He's never going to marry you.

But she was absolutely right.

Let's go, let's meet in Santiago de Compostela, where it will rain and rain and rain, a woman will rent us a room and rattle the door handle every two hours to make us come out during the day, saying, You can't stay in bed, I've rented you the room only for sleeping. And we will have to go outdoors and walk and walk and walk in the rain; the poor saints on the cathedral walls will be all covered with lichen and moss, stone made smooth by water and fog, this is the rainiest part of the continent, and we will go into a bar to dry out, to warm up, and we will drink hot chocolate made with heavy thick cream that is sweet, so sweet, that it is like drinking a melted bar of chocolate with a dollop of whipped cream.

Folors
Fo ma sospeissos
A foolish thing was my presumption.

But then it was so different.

All the debates about a life devoted to activism, social justice, revolution-versus-a-life-devoted-to-art. Which would it be, which would it be?

You could plead rock'n'roll. They forgive the troubadour anything, even if he likes really expensive cars.

You were granted a certain dispensation.

You didn't have to picket the governor's mansion, you didn't have to wash out bottles and cans for recycling, you didn't have to engage in a discourse on the ethics of private property or the way in which women are objectified repressed and silenced by a culture dominated by white middle-aged men.

Middle age. We're getting close now, aren't we, depending on how long you think you're going to live. What's your actuarial prediction? It must not be so long for rock'n'rollers, even those devoted to lyrics, but I imagine that since you've made it to forty, this has significantly increased the chances that you will live to old age, whereas, at age nineteen or twenty, it was a very risky proposition. I, myself, keep upping the ante; I'm at eighty now. But by the next big milestone, the floating halfway point, the middle of my life's path will have to be shifted upward again, extending my life to ninety. This I can imagine and still avoid calling myself middle-aged. But after that, it gets tricky, the revising upward. One hundred? I am reluctant to push it so high. Do I want to live to one hundred and twenty, like Jeanne Louise Calment of Arles, the lady in the newspaper who gave up cigarettes at ninety-five because she could not suffer the indignity of not being able to light them herself? At some point soon, I will be middle aged, but you? Another dispensation? You could always get them. You said twenty was your middle point, but you were not correct in your sensitive young man poet projections.

Your stature, you were tall on top of it, aloof, allowed you to be part of the discourse yet kept you out of the conflicts. But me, I was pounced on, sitting in that living room chair, inhaling a Marlboro, hoping to outdistance migraine. How can you think of art, of literature, when there are so many starving people, so many tortured prisoners? someone started in on me. I had said I was thinking of going to graduate school in French. Someone asked if that meant I would then go to French-speaking Africa to do hunger work. I said, no, no, if I am very very lucky, I'll get to teach French grammar and literature at a Big Ten university.

The literature of the French Revolution. Richard Fallon said this, and began to lecture everyone else. He was wearing his navy blue proletarian seaman's cap.

He was talking about the evolution of the French Revolution. The lessons of the French Revolution. The betrayal of the French Revolution. This is what she will be dedicated to.

He said it as if he had bailed me out of an ideological fix, some reactionary hole I had dug myself into as a result of inarticulateness. That made me resist. *Liberté. Égalité.* I said I didn't foresee myself concentrating on the French Revolution.

Richard Fallon was stunned silent.

I love the lyric poetry, I said.

Elaine Leonardi called me bourgeois and elitist. She always carried the torch for you. She worked herself up into a self-righteous little frenzy and said, Don't you think you'll find it irrelevant to be counting out syllables while babies in Third World countries are dying from dehydration because multinational corporations are forcing baby formula down their throats?

At that point everyone else mumbled in agreement and drifted off to other parts of the room. Mark Robinson flipped through a stack of albums leaning against the wall next to the television set and picked out Bob Marley. *Lively up yourself because I said so.*

This was his way of defusing the situation.

Patricia Early filled up a bong with water at the kitchen sink.

William Krebs chopped up dill pickles and made himself a tunafish sandwich.

My eye sockets hurt I was so stung. There was an empty Grain Belt on the arm of the sofa and I picked it up and started to peel off the label.

Did you know Elaine Leonardi was diagnosed with breast cancer two years ago; she is a nurse and works in an AIDS clinic in Humbolt Park in Chicago.

Richard Fallon, most radical man, is a lawyer for Disney, dedicated to the Disneyfication of Europe. I saw him at a wedding at a country club not too long ago.

We were standing underneath a crystal chandelier in the center of a ballroom with parquet floors. I was holding a glass of Pinot Grigio, trying to catch the eye of the waitress who was serving jumbo shrimp marinated in soy sauce and ginger and sesame seeds.

He said, My work is an extension of the revolution, the left extends so far it becomes the right and forms a circle.

Yes, Richard, I said. It's all become Mickey and Donald.

Yes, exactly, he said.

So, see what you missed. You had to go and become a rock star. I'm sorry, I know you are not a star-star, you are an anti-star, a reclusive one who gives no interviews, and frankly no one asks that often, you're a musician's musician. But oh, I have not thought of you for such a very long time; I have two children, one miscarriage behind me. A near-divorce. I was a landlady, but we have no tenants now because we took over the upstairs apartment. I am teaching at a small Catholic college and every other year I get to teach my course on Troubadour Lyric Poetry. I have not thought of you in a very long time, but when the tune tumbled out of the speakers, I knew from the first few glycerine chords that it was you. After the tire bounced off the curb, I pulled the van over next to the park and I listened. I listened, I suppose, to see if there would be me in there somewhere. I could not hear your voice distinctly; it was the ageless angels who were coming through. How futile to envy angels, but sometimes I do. I listened to the words and there was something in each line. The lyrics were obscure and slightly out-of-reach, the melody was halting, and I remember thinking for a second, is he playing a guitar or lute?

I don't want you thinking I have been walking around for the past twenty years mooning after you. No. It is very, very far away, those very early dawns. Very sweet and sad. But it came upon me like a thwack, unexpected and painful.

Thwack. There you were.

> Now, it behooves me to think on something else,
> for I love such a one to whom I make no entreaty
> because in the thinking itself I know well I'm at fault.

What shall I do? for a bold urge comes to me
that I should go and plead
then fear makes me renounce it.
E paors fai m'o lasser.

⁂

I read somewhere that Neil Young cut his finger while trying to slice open a package of turkey wrapped in sealed-tight plastic and he had to change his plans. Has that ever happened to you?

⁂

A penas sai comensar
un ver que volh far leuger . . .
I hardly know how to begin a poem
which I want to make light and easy.

Yes, this was always a problem. I could never make myself easy.

⁂

Tunes! someone howled a long time ago, in a living room where there was silence. We need tunes!

⁂

You need the rub, you need the wound,
otherwise the line is just too smooth,
your song came through the speakers.

⁂

Minstrel, now, I say to you, with these new tunes be off.

Noli Me Tangere

See how close people come, drawn to the same spot, crowding her, closing in. A handful of viewers in this ample room, six, and all are hovering. There are other famous paintings, other Titians to choose from, *Bacchus and Ariadne, Portrait of a Man, The Vendramin Family,* but here they are, swarming around her, pressing toward the very painting she looks into. Her skin itches, they are so close. If they would just space themselves out evenly across the designated viewing area, there would be no discomfort. There would be no pressing. She could better tolerate someone stepping in front and blocking her view, than she can the shoulder bag that brushes now against her elbow.

Can they not read? It says right there on the brass plate that names the painting, *Noli Me Tangere.* Do not touch me.

Time added up, year after year. Five years without time off. If it could have kept accruing, she would never have touched it. She would have left it there, like money in the bank. But if you do not use it by a certain time, it is taken away. Poof. Gone. And she is enough of an immigrant to know that you do not let a thing out of your hand if you have worked for it. If you have worked for it, it is yours. She earned these days, hoarded them. One year worked meant two weeks of vacation time. Two years meant three more. And so on. The days in accumulation gave her pain, but also certain comfort, comfort that her discontent was earned. There it was, printed twice a month on her paycheck stub. Most people spend every single day due them, and the days are gone by the end of the year. She takes a certain pleasure in knowing she is not profligate with her days, that she does not spend them unless she needs them, and that she does not need them.

Her father and mother mock the office workers in the city with their regular vacations. *We were put on this earth to work, not to waste hours changing the color of our skin at the beach.* How stern they are, how tight. Work, work, work. Saturdays and Sundays, too. When she was a teenager, all she wanted was to sit on the sofa reading without her mother walking in and saying, What are you doing?

Her mother, so healthy and strong. Every day she goes to clean houses, though she no longer needs to. Their house is paid off. Her father has his pension. Her mother, as if she cannot see herself in her daughter, says, You go and go and go and go.

At work, someone finds out how much time is stored up. You haven't taken a vacation in how long? She was teased, ribbed, needled, by attendings, residents, medical technicians. Pressure, constant pressure. Then a nurse with a sister in a travel agency started in. Take a little trip, she said. Relax. Rest. Bargain fares to Manila. Not Manila? Okay, Jamaica, then. Acapulco. No, she said. Mind your own business, Carmen.

At four A.M. one morning, she was standing at the nurses' station looking over charts. The hallway was nearly empty. An insomniac patient in a powder blue gown walked down the corridor pulling along an i.v. pole, dragging her right leg from back to front. A stiff post-partum gait, an epidural wearing off. Coffee? a nice looking junior colleague asked her, startled her, boom, yanking her out of her assessing. Do you want to have breakfast? She fumbled, blushed. No. Thanks. I have a lot of work to do.

He said, You're not one much for spontaneity are you?

By noon, she had spoken to Carmen. Carmen had spoken with her sister. A ticket to London. Hotel room and eight plays. Leave two days from tomorrow. Fine.

London? her mother said. You're finally taking off time from work and travelling across the ocean, and it's not to Italy where you have people?

But here she stands in London, in a gallery with burgundy-red walls, in the space before a painting, staring at a flat surface when a glint of white pricks her eye, like a twig scraping it. The crisp white is on a piece of cloth; she swallows, squints, and leans, leans, until tap, she is gently barred by the velvet cordon that brushes against her shin. Do not touch. The painting itself orders it, *Noli Me Tangere.* Yet everything else demands the opposite: the gauze of Mary Magdalene's billowing sleeves, the barely veiled flesh of her plump upper arm, the cushioned grooves in the folds of her gown, the train behind her that caresses the ground. The color of her gown? Red, of course, crimson. Raw silk that begs to be touched, begs you to bury your face in it. And Christ's garment? A shroud, glinting ice-white, is wound around his lower torso, his navel exposed, a smooth hairless belly. It is tossed up and draped over his shoulders, tied into an efficient knot at the top of his sternum. He bows slightly, away from Mary Magdalene, pulls the winding cloth just out of her reach and sweeps himself away from her gracefully.

Letizia Mattei takes in the painting in broad and narrow sweeps. Christ holding a gardener's hoe. Mary Magdalene's fingers nearly touching the ground, wrapped around the alabaster ointment jar. Christ emerged from the cave, but the cave nowhere in sight.

Her eyes dart from foreground to background. Center. A risen Christ standing. On the right, Mary Magdalene, extending her hand to his. Behind them, a sunrise. The sun has not yet shown itself above the horizon line, the sea is off in the distance. The light of the sunrise begins white below the clouds, a rosy-white, a butter-yellow. A shimmer, a dazzle, a buffed light. Above the golden clouds, the sky is blue, a blue her mother calls *l'azzurro d'Italia,* Italian blue, as if a place can make exclusive claim to color. The sea is a band of deeper blue below the horizon. In the upper right corner of the canvas, below the sky and above the sea, there is a farmhouse. A farmhouse perched on a hill. But it is not a house of the sea coast, with red tiled roof and stucco walls, but an inland house of the mountains, with walls of slab-grey stone.

Letizia Mattei, researcher and clinician, makes an observation: *There is an inland house placed above the sea. Mary Magdalene and Christ wear clothes of different centuries. Time out of place, place out of time.*

To the left, behind Christ's head, is a sunlit pasture, below it a green field with sheep. Up, down, left, right, her eyes skitter.

On the right, above the figures in the foreground, is a man, a tiny stick figure walking down a hill. Tall and lanky, all angles. Charcoal-grey splotches of paint and three dashes of white.

Her eyes dart up. In front of the stone house, there is an arched entryway. And in front of the farmhouse, the threshing floor. Her grandfather's house was called La Gruccia. Above, an abandoned fortress with massive blocks of tumbled stone.

※

Mary Magdalene's arm is outstretched to touch the back of Christ's hand with her fingertip and for a split second, Doctor Letizia Mattei feels herself lurch forward. But the momentary lunge is jolted, stop, and she finds herself gesturing, not with Mary Magdalene, but with the recoiling Christ, his body wrapping itself up in his white garment, pulling it away from a reaching hand.

When she looked at Michelangelo's painting in another room, she was not affected this way. It did not make her want to touch clothing or skin; she was bumped back and away, oriented and comfortable as soon as her familiar habit of analysis could resume. She examined the sinew, the musculature; it withstood her scrutiny, it was a brilliantly accurate depiction. She studied the plasticity of the folds in the garments. But it did not make her want to extend her arm to touch the canvas the way this one does.

She looks at Christ's face, his benign, benevolent, perpetually understanding face, and what she sees is a wince. As if there is nothing he would like better than to clasp Mary Magdalene's hand.

She did not think she would end up like this, turning forty.

She has dedicated her life to neurotransmitters. To dopamine and serotonin. She knows how newborn monkeys die from lack of touch, how they turn on themselves and gnaw.

She knows how cells communicate with one another, that axons shoot out forward, that the message is not carried whole over the course of its journey, and it is only when these broken parts of message converge somewhere downstream, that a whole image can be assembled momentarily.

It is the modulator neurons Letizia Mattei is concerned with, the ones that make synapse possible.

Snap, crackle, pop. This is how her mother describes her work.

Her mother brags. We are so very proud of her. A specialist of the nerves. She researches. She cures. She works with the poor people.

In the backyard in the summer, at a barbecue for her father's birthday: Letizia flies everywhere to present her research.

Then, that evening, in the long-lingering daylight, while they were in the kitchen washing plastic spoons and forks at the kitchen sink, her mother said,

Why don't you see about a job somewhere closer? At that beautiful hospital, Northwestern, right there on the lake. Or at Loyola? That's closer. You've gotten awards; don't you think you would have a chance?

Ma, Letizia Mattei said. I have the job I want.

Okay, okay. *Se vuoi far quel lavoro lì.* If that's the kind of work you want, fine, I won't say another word about it.

The poor people. The ones who are most desperate.

Quell' gente disperata.

Mendicanti e vagabondi.

Beggars and vagabonds.

We were never beggars, her mother said. We knew how to work for a living.

Every single morning, she beats the traffic by leaving home at six o'clock. She is always home by nine. She rents an apartment right there at the intersection of Berteau and Damen. Rent keeps going up, but she is settled there.

Her father talks of equity. Of paying all that money out in rent. You should buy something, we could help you out.

Maybe next year, Pa.

Next year and next year and next year, he said, muttering under his breath. *L'an' cl'arriva l'è ne mia promess' a nessun.* Next year is promised to no one.

In the morning, she sometimes she sees her cousin walking along Damen Avenue farther south to catch the el. He walks along, tall, lanky, all angles, his hooked nose, reading the paper as he ambles, the image of nonchalance, smoking his Marlboro cigarette. She offered once to take him to a laboratory to show him a dissected lung, but he jabbed her shoulder, told her he'd take a rain check. He is a litigator, making lots of money. He too is wasting his money on rent, but he gets to live where there is night-life, and has a ping-pong table in his living room.

Her cousin tells her, You rely too much on your brain, and where has it gotten you? You're sure not having any fun.

Every few months, she sees him walking along. She honks, he looks up startled, then she sees him waving, a tiny paint-dropped man, in her rear-view mirror.

She had not intended to take a vacation alone.

If she conceptualized loneliness as a disease, she would think of her situation diagnostically. If her problem were a skin ailment it would be difficult to diagnose because there are no marks indicating this inability to tolerate touch. No obvious lesions, nodules, wheals. No scabs or scars. True, she bites her nails, and the skin around her fingers is raw and sometimes bleeds. She chews the inside of her mouth which gives her a strange sense of pleasure. She will sometimes scratch the skin on her hand if there is already a sore there. But what causes the itching? There is no bacterial or parasitic infection. Dermatitis? Caused by what? The sun? An allergy? Psychogenic factors? that is to say, factors related to the mind? But Letizia Mattei does not believe in the mind, only the brain.

She looks again at the skin of the hands in the painting. Is this why Christ pushes Mary Magdalene away, because he has some type of dermatitis and fears that his skin would flake off if it were in the least way stimulated?

Maybe the whole reason for the painting, the farmhouse, the sea, the hill with the man descending, is that Titian was thinking about skin disease, that he had seen children with skin infected by ringworm. Ringworm, *tinea* in medical terms. In Italian, *tignia*, which is also a name for someone who is annoying, stingy, mean, and Letizia knows that *tignia* has the same tight sound as the middle part of her name.

Thoughts tumble out one after another in divergent lines, in tangents. The painting has undone her ordered brain and there is no system to her viewing and her thinking. Maybe Titian painted this because he was afraid of contagion, *contagion,* another word with touch implied, *con* and *tangere*. He would have feared contagion; he would have feared a hand touching a hand. The cyclical patterns of influenza, plague. They all went out with gloves, those who could afford them. Even in Italy today, when the cashier gives back change, money is slid into a tray, not dropped into a customer's hand as it is in democratic America, where it is an insult not to place money directly into someone's hand. Fear of contagion has outlasted the plague. Titian died from the plague as a very old man, ninety or more, and he painted the painting when he was young. Perhaps Titian was considering disease and contagion and touch. But he was hardly a man who abhorred touch. Just look at Mary Magdalene's skin; it seems illuminated from inside.

What if it is not a skin disease that affects Letizia Mattei? What if it is the perineurium which is defective, the connective sheath that surrounds a bundle of nerve fibers? Maybe it is a neurological defect that leaves her impervious to touch.

And if it is not the skin or the neurological system at fault, then what about clinical depression, which is what someone who passed through her life, before he was banished, suggested. She scoffed. Depression is in the mind. A disease of the idle. As she stares at the painting, she remembers her reply to him, Depression is a disease for those with time in their hands, embarrassed again, a thousand miles away, by the lapse in her word choice. Time in their hands. She emigrated at eleven and speaks without an accent but there are, infrequent and subtle, slips.

Her eyes are ultramarine. When patients see her eyes, then see the name embroidered into her white coat as she leans over to take a pulse, the joke, *The milkman was a Swede. Ha. Ha.*

She did not know she loved him then. They pulled away and pushed against one another until their skin ached. Now she sleeps, infrequently, with a married man.

One night, at midnight, she sat in a chair in the lounge, the sound of the television turned down. There was no work, but she could not sleep. She flipped through a magazine. An article in which the successful son of an immigrant discusses success. Such a festive people.

Musical. Warm. Boisterous. Emotional. Singing! Dancing! Food! Such a sociable people, completely unable to tolerate solitude, the successful man said. She threw down the magazine onto the coffee table. We are people of the mountains who do not waste anything, expend anything unnecessarily. Words. Gestures. We are hermetic in our stone houses, and in the spring we must teach ourselves to speak again.

In the cafeteria line a month ago, she overheard two nurses up ahead of her in line. One said, *She thinks nobody knows but everyone does.* The other one said, *He's not going to leave his wife.* The first one said, *They never do.* Doctor Letizia Mattei grabbed her empty tray, walked to a table in the corner and faced the wall.

Christ in the painting says Do Not Touch Me, but yearns for contact. Contact, another word related to touch. *Con* and *tangere,* like *contagion.* Like *tangent.* Like the tangent of her thought process as she stares at the painting, thoughts not normally associated with one another brushing against one another, glancing off each other. She is not normally like this. She has an orderly mind. She insists on it. She does not dream. She does not believe in dreams. She does not daydream. If she begins to think vaguely, she stops herself. There is too much work to be idle. She earns her living by avoiding tangents. She is expert in making rational explanation of what occurs between synapse and tic. She does not value stream-of-consciousness; thought is organic, can be explained by the chemical composition of mechanoreceptors, and yet, here she stands in front of a painting five hundred years old, fatigued, digressing, on a tangent, trying to decide whether she is more like Christ or Mary Magdalene. She recognizes she is tachycardiac. She is diaphoretic. Of all things, she does not want to lose control. She does not want her thoughts swarming. *I should be dealing with this better.* She does not want her senses to overtake her brain, yet, more than anything in the world, she wants to press the palm of her hand flat against the canvas. She has read about this syndrome, which is not a medical syndrome, so she does not believe it exists. Fainting, dizziness, rapid heart beat, the result of too much stimulation, Stendahl's syndrome, and she is stunned to see it happening to her, this acute dissociation. There, she thinks, yet another word that has to do with touch, *association*. From *ad* and *sociare*, to join, from *socius*, companion. Her father calls his friends *soci*. Associates. Pals. This tangent, so out of character. She does not weep. She thinks that crying is for the weak. *We are a strong people.* Her mentor, a pediatrician, said she wept when she saw Michelangelo's *David*. Doctor Letizia Mattei thought her melodramatic, histrionic, art is art, life is life, adamant, but here she is now, staring at a painting, exhausted, and she feels a hard knot in her throat, a tiny choke-pear, as she looks into the background and sees far off from the main drama of the canvas, the tiny stick man, who walks down a dirt slope with his dog, a paint-dropped man, Giacometti-thin. Made of unconnected dots. Of synapses. Who is this man who has receded so much into memory that the artist painted him so distantly? Including him though he had nothing to do with the central drama of the painting? Who is this angular being walking alone, lanky, all knees and elbows, his dog bounding ahead of him, walking down a hill toward a pasture of lamb-white sheep, toward the tiny field, the one yielding *campo* that has been plowed and planted? Who is this man the painter included, a tangent to the subject at hand, which is the space where touch does not occur.

Shards

etizia Mattei, Letizia Mattei, you have come here almost too late. What an American you have become, now, demanding a tour. Click. Click. Follow me.

Watch your head as you step in, the entryway is low. Follow me. It will take your eyes a few minutes to adjust to the dark. A miserable spring day, isn't it? The thirteenth of April, feast day of San Martín, you know, he gave a beggar his cloak. A miserable spring day, spitting snow up here in these mountains. Everything grey, no color, we are so, so tired of waiting. One more second for your eyes to adjust. Now, follow me here, to the center. No flash, please.

The light comes in obliquely, on an angle, enters through two narrow slits in the northeast part of the cavern's dome. It falls in two shafts, hitting a depression in the center of the pavement, a concave stone embedded in the ground.

Squint Letizia, squint, see if you can't focus a little better. It is a miserable April day, and the light that enters is dim.

For ten thousand *lire* I will light the candles, her guide says. He wears a sheepskin vest that hangs to just below his waist. He is a tall, slight man, whose clothes hang loosely, and he must have once been massive.

Or for five thousand, he says, you can light them yourself.

His voice is water rumbling over river stones. Like stones knocking against one another underwater.

It will only be a few more moments, he says, looking upward toward the dome. Letizia Mattei sees a long-faced man with a jutting chin, vertical creases that stretch down the side of his face. Beardless. They are about the same height.

※

He turns to her and says, I recognize you, you look somehow familiar.

As they stand in the dark, he says, You work as a doctor I understand. People here talk, what can I say? A specialist of the nerves and brain? Very good, very good. But it seems to me there are some questions that books will never answer.

He laughs a gravel-gurgling laugh.

※

Only a few more seconds, he says. Unless you want me to go ahead and light the candles. Yes?

Click.

Letizia Mattei's eyes are stung by the sudden explosion of light.

Did you think I was going to use matches? No, this is the modern age. You travellers think we're still living back during the days of Count Montecuccoli, no running water, no light. We have enough electricity for a lifetime. You all come here looking for a place out of time, so you can slow the pace of your days.

In this flood of light, Letizia Mattei sees the man has ice-blue eyes, sees something familiar in the leather-tooled creases around them, in the high-boned cheeks that are permanently wind-burned.

❧

Letizia Mattei stands in a cavern, looking up at a dome, at an oval covered with mosaic: a turtle crawling onto a golden shore and a palm tree. The oval in the center of this golden dome is surrounded by a field of magnificent blue.

❧

Click. Now, the northern wall is completely lit, a-jumble with fresco and mosaic. The electric lights give off a whitish light that illuminates ten distinct partitions. Her eyes go upward toward the painted figure of a naked man who has strings attached from neck to hands, hip to ankle, making him looked winged, or else like a marionette. In fourteen spots around this body, neck and ears, armpits, flanks, groin and knees, there are perfectly round splotches of black, swollen darkened circles, which she recognizes at once as buboes, or the swelling points of lymph nodes, where signs of certain illnesses first appear, lymphatic cancer, bubonic plague.

In these cases, the arc of illness is swift.

Swifter than any stag, my days have fled like shadows.

Drip, drip, drip, drip. Second by second into her mother's veins.

❧

The complex of elements that form the base of the nervous reflex system is called the arc. She is an expert in the particles that form this arc. She works tirelessly, obsessively, with enormous concentration. At work they joke that she is a mule, about her ability to just keep pulling and pulling and walking day after day, she is so dogged and persistent. She studies the connection between brain cells, the relationship between synapse and twitch.

Oh Letizia, Letizia, as if neuroanatomy can save you.
First, do no harm.

Under the arch that covers one wall, every square inch is covered with fresco or mosaic, and the electric brightness is too much.
Turn off the lights, please, she says. I'll pay to light the candles.

Whatever you want, some of you Americans have to do everything the hard way. Click. Click. And the cavern is dark again.
You'll have to use the ladder to light the candles, he says. I'm too old to go climbing around up there.
No, it's fine. Don't worry. I'll do it, Letizia Mattei says.

One by one she lights the candles of the northern wall, igniting all the colors:
Yellows made from broom and buckthorn, camomile and salvia.
Vermilion and crimson.

Greens made from the juice of certain berries and from terre-verte dug out of the mountainside.

The cheeks of the angels are a buttery-pink.

The blue that surrounds the dome is a blue beyond both sky and sea.

⁂

As she lights the candles, one by one saints Gioacchino, Bernar-dino, Pellegrino emerge. In other partitions, she sees prisoners with hands raised high, a woman begging with palms uplifted, refugees carrying loads on their backs, a burning book.

⁂

She turns to face the opposite wall. She lights the candles one by one. Again, ten partitions under an arch. Seven have no color and the figures are merely trails of dashes, spindly and thin, like Giacometti's people, how do they manage to stand upright? The figures are painted with a black made from acorn husks, a brown made from walnuts, corrosive pigment that has faded.

Did the artist run out of color? she asks her guide.

Ma chi sa, he replies. Who knows.

In the other partitions: a man hands a cloak to another; a man converses with one who is chained to a wall; one man speaks to a woman on her deathbed; one man prepares food in a pot hanging over a fire in a fireplace; one woman drops coins, plunk, plunk, into the jar of a seated beggar; one man drops particles onto a slab of stone that is marked with a cross. These depictions of consolation, the Seven Works of Mercy, are completely devoid of color.

In the three remaining partitions, however, there is color: a golden threshing floor with plentiful golden grain; two long-legged heron-blue cranes drinking from a fountain; and in the uppermost panel at the top of the arch, a tipped-over jar from which cascade glittering fragments of colored stone, glistening like jewels, and tiny pieces of mirror.

⚹

Ma, in her pantry, kept jars of broken glasses, and cups, and vases, and bowls, intending to put them back together. When I have time. In the meantime, don't throw anything away, bring it to me. I'll take care of it. *Ci penso io.*

In the pantry, straight ahead, on the top shelf. Jars and jars full of little broken pieces.

⚹

It's the ointment jar of Mary Magdalene, he says pointing to the picture of the jar above. He shines his flashlight way up to the top.

See, do you see it?

Yes. A small rectangular panel, a painting within a painting, almost hidden, it is so small and dark against the rest of the mosaic, a depiction of two figures, one-dimensional, in profile, stiff, motionless. A man stands holding a gardener's hoe, a woman on her knees reaches toward him, but they do not touch. Mary Magdalene and Christ in the garden, and in the background, the jagged horizon is a chain of mountains. The contents of the enormous ointment jar fall, pieces of broken mirror that glitter, plump drops that fall into partitions below, two or three shards of mirror into each frame. Letizia Mattei stands on the ladder and lights the candles, each of which sits on a tiny stone shelf. She climbs back down to sees how colors have emerged in the mosaic above.

You know, you look familiar, like someone I knew once, and yet

230

I cannot place you, her guide says to her. The Mattei were always smart, too smart for their own good; the men always married the prettiest girls and the girls always married the most hard-working men. You look smart like the rest of them, so you probably would be interested in this little booklet we have here to sell; it's not too long, but it gives you information about this cave, more than I can give, written by some professor down in Modena. This cave is not consecrated, and some of the experts say it is not authentic. Still, there are some studious types who pay attention to it, but I think they just make one big muddle with all of their opinions.

Yes, Letizia Mattei says, I would like to buy a copy.

It's another ten thousand lire.

That's fine, she says. I'll take it.

She opens the flap of a small pouch that hangs from a strap that crosses her body. The purse is bulging with crumpled bills of every size. She fumbles through it, finds another ten thousand lire note.

He stuffs the money into his pocket, hands her the small booklet. The paper of the cover is chalky, there is nothing glossy or smooth about it. On the cover is an ink drawing of three heads, each floating above wings that are shaped like boats. She opens at random:

Semi-precious stones, a ruby, garnets, and rare fragments of colored glass that have the distinct markings of hand-blown glass made by Venetian glassmakers, are embedded into the mosaic. How he would have come into possession of these stones is difficult to imagine. Similarly, how to explain the ultramarine?

In the low-lit cave, Letizia Mattei reads.

Contents tumble from the ointment jar, spilling and dropping like plump coins, to consolatory images below. These drops glisten, each drop embedded into the mosaic, sometimes in an eye. On the innermost row of the southern wall, is a farmhouse, its window lit with yellow paint. In the foreground, lies a disproportionately large threshing floor, the ara, *as it is called in these mountains, and laid atop the* ara *are three enormous stalks of a plant that resembles wheat. Clearly, this image refers to the image opposite it on the northern wall, where a woman with outstretched hands depicts hunger.*

And beneath this depiction are the letters, I N C O, *faded and barely legible, whose meaning is not clear, perhaps a misinformed attempt on the part of an illiterate who tried to reproduce the letters traditionally painted at the top of Christ's cross,* I N H S.

Inco is something she knows but where is it stored in her brain?

Although we have the illusion that everything comes together in a single anatomical location, images are not put together in one specific anatomical site. There is no single region of the brain equipped to simultaneously process representations from all the sensory modalities. In all likelihood the relative simultaneity of activity at different sites binds the separate images together. She has recently spoken these words in a lecture to medical students. The brain does not store images whole; there is no storage room full of paintings, stacked against a wall. The brain stores parts of images, which it can reassemble, put back together, to render the whole, complete image.

✨

She lights the candles of the western wall, which is divided vertically into seven partitions, the seven days of creation. A fourth partition spans the door. To the left of the door, small straight lines are painted in rows, as if someone had kept count of the days.

✨

We are a simple people, her mother said. We work each day, we die. Our happiest times are when our children are small. I did not mind cleaning houses; it's what I did. I did not mistake myself for them, the *signori* for the servant. My happiest time was when you were small, I did not mind working hard, you always did something to make me proud. I was never embarrassed by this work, I was making a better life for you, and we were never beggars.

※

Tending your sick. *I tuoi malati,* her mother called them. Your sick ones.

If you had as much time for us as you do for them.

※

With every passing year, researchers are able to look at smaller and smaller particles to see what makes connections, what leaps from the tether-tail of one neuron to another.

Images are probably the main contents of thought, regardless of the sensory modality in which they are generated; this, the basis of her research.

Images are probably the main content of thought.

Cain pummels Abel. Thwack. Over and over and over.

Isaac's neck is stretched and smooth, ready for the sacrifice.

Eve cowers, her torso writhes.

Over and over and over.

These the images in the brains of those little babies.

Thwack. Crack. Cower. Hunger-gnaw.

How do those circuits form and re-form?

How are messages sent? Bleep. Interruption.

Pummel. Blast. Tear. Then deaden-numb.

Neurons fire. Misfire. Fizzle unconnected.

Early exposure to violence, stress and other environmental pressures can cause the brain to run on fast track, increasing the risk of impulsive emotions and high blood pressure. What happens to the neurotransmitter serotonin when a child's hears, Blam! sees his mother or father, brother or sister, fall into a crumpled heap?

My mother kept me safe.

Mental images are momentary constructions.

Her finger against her mother's eyelid, the skin did not stay in place but folded over itself, slackened, she was surprised, unnerved. Her mother's skin was not young. Letizia Mattei in front of the bathroom mirror with her mother, touching her mother's eyelid, applying eye powder, colored dust, which her mother never wore, but she was going to a wedding, and she had asked her daughter, How do you put this stuff on anyway?

Letizia Mattei lights candles on the eastern wall, which is opposite the door.

Are you sure you don't want me to turn on the lights back on? he asks. It's getting late.

No, if it's all right, I'll just finish.

She lights a wall with three panels. She expects to see God the Father, God the Son, and God the Holy Ghost. Instead, there are three heads with halos, severe expressions, and underneath each head are wings that are shaped like a boat.

This vault is not consecrated, he says, so there's no money for its upkeep.

He says to her, I'm a little tired. I'm going to sit on the bench outside. Here, I'll leave you my flashlight.

※

Letizia Mattei steps under the shafts of light and holds the flashlight above the booklet:

Stark and uninviting, their gazes at once overbearing, unbearable, and vulnerable. It is unclear whether they represent angels, the Trinity, or three separate godheads.

Letizia Mattei shifts the flashlight to the other hand, trying to steady the beam of light.

Those fleeing persecutions fled up into these mountains. Christians fleeing Romans. Romans fleeing Northmen. Jews fleeing persecution in the cities below. Heretics fled here, those accused of being "Lutheran," many unknowing that they had become heretics: Does not it say Light from Light, there in your book? one miller unflinchingly told his Inquisitors, and from this premise concluded that God is Light.

※

A screeching hinge startles her. Her guide has come back in.

I need to warm up my hands, he says. He blows into his hands.

I told you, he says, there are some things you can't find in a book. For two summers they all came up to look at the cave. Ooh and ahh. Magnifying glasses and cameras, they measured and they touched. They couldn't all fit inside. Some professors in Florence dispute the cave's authenticity, they would of course, they've never given the mountain people their due, but there is a smaller group from Modena that believes it's real. The town gives me a little something to sit here each day in the summer in case a tourist shows up. The rest of the year, you have to come and find me. I've worked on my feet all my life, so I don't mind spending my final days sitting down. That booklet can give you some ideas about the cave, but I can tell you something that's not in the book.

When I was a boy, my mother always said, Never go up there! Never go up near the caves! We talked about other places in the same tone, a place down past the foothills, where hundreds were killed. They made them dig their own graves, then shot them in the back of the head, and they fell into the pits they had dug. And Marzabotto down there on the plains was not the only place. Just pick up the newspaper, just watch the television as you sit there eating your dinner.

And so, whenever I said, What is up there? I was steered away from it: It's wilderness, it's wild, there's no reason to go near there. Years and years of mothers telling children, Never, never, ever, go near there. Without saying why. Why? Oh no reason, there is absolutely nothing there to find, just do not go near there. Even the brawny, strapping men, and the most fearless, toothless old woman, did not go near there. Centuries passed. And when it was found by two young lovers, foreigners, looking for a private space, it was rediscovered. The debate started.

No, one said. Leave the past alone. We have only now begun to heal. Our children do not remember, why should we ignite old and terrible wounds, tear them open again?

Yes, we must see what is in the cave, another one said. The truth must eventually come out. The truth. We must face it. If there are remains, then we must see them. We must see what we have done to one another to prevent it from happening again.

Someone sued to keep it closed.

Someone sued to have it opened.

The area was sealed off. A guard was posted day and night.

Once long ago, three men went missing and were never seen again. They were fleeing to the other side of the line, heading toward the new Republic in the town founded by the followers of St. Benedict. Made to hold their hands up, executed, their bodies flung into a pit, a cave. A band of them, disappeared forever. You read about the wars now, you see the same pictures.

Should the cave be uncovered? Must we look inside?

The questions divided husband from wife, father from son, sister from sister, teacher from pupil. They all argued:

Just when life was easing up, we have to go digging up the ugly period?

The collaborators are ancient, almost all the *fuorusciti* who fled and hid up in the mountains, are dead. Why, why, dredge it all up again? Leave it be. We'll scare away the tourists.

Fuck the tourists, with their Range Rovers and plates from Toscana. FI. Firenze. PI. Pisa. LU. Lucca. The Americans wearing Reeboks. The truth is more important.

The tourists will go somewhere else. You think they won't go somewhere else? just a few miles away, over to the next valley? They'll taste metal in the water. This is a poor zone, tourism is all that we have. If it weren't for them, how much more would the population shrink?

And so the debate continued for two years, the area, inaccessible by auto, cordoned off, a guard stationed twenty-four hours a day. Of course they hired an outsider, and didn't give the job to someone from around here.

The caves, some said, were the hiding places of Jews during the war.

We hid them and risked our lives, some said, bragging now after a generation. We brought them food and water for the better part of four years. What they don't say is that they made them pay.

Others whispered that the caves were mass graves.

The collaborators made the old man walk very far on the road above, then they made him dig his own grave.

Then the partisans made the old man walk very far on the road above, and they made him dig his own grave.

We saved the Jews, some bragged.

There were no Jews up here in the mountains, others countered, they were all down in the cities.

We were heroes and we were brave. Now after it is over, everyone is a hero and a rebel.

All we tried to do was survive, you think first of your own. They make their apologies in this way.

Long ago, they rounded up entire villages of men and they herded them up into the mountains, and the men disappeared, and nobody remembered them aloud. No one remembered or could say exactly where the caves were, only that they were *over there somewhere, up there.*

Others, more refined in their imaginings, said paintings were hidden there. That the humidity and temperature in the caves would have been perfect, that the Germans would have known this. Didn't the Germans spend years garrisoned in a house on the road that passes above Ardonlà? Some said, buried below, was a famous, untraceable Titian.

When they opened the cave, no one from the towns nearby came, it was only those from outside. That professor from Modena who wrote the little book was among them. I myself was not. I was afraid of what would be found. Bones and teeth.

But that is not what they found, maybe in some other place, definitely in some other place, you only need to watch the television while you're eating leftovers. All those years, everybody afraid to look, forgetting what was there. They found frescoes and mosaics. We do not deserve this consolation, we do not deserve it at all, but I'll take it anyway.

※

I know who you are, he says to her. *Mi gnosc mia?* You don't know me?

No, I'm afraid, I don't.

What was your grandmother's name?

She answers a name.

No, the other grandmother.

Giovanna. Mordini.

Before she became Mordini.

Bartolai. Did you know her?

He laughs. His laugh a low rumble, a gurgle.

※

And you? she asks him. What is your name?

First or last? First, last, it doesn't make a difference, they call me Zacagnèr, just like they called my father before me. Your grandmother was a Bartolai before she went off and married Mordini. Mordini had three different fields. He was not destined to wander the world like the rest of us. Mordini had three fields, and all I had were mules. I knew your grandmother, she was going to marry me, but then she went off and married Mordini instead. Lucky for you.

※

INCO? she says to Zacagnèr.

You don't remember such a basic word? You, who are supposed to be so smart.

I hear it in my brain, she says, but I don't know what it means.

Inco, he says. Today. This day. The word that is written above the Seven Acts of Mercy.

※

Sopra l'ara la giornada l'è ammazzà, Zacagnèr says. Upon the altar the day is slain.

It's a saying here in Ardonlà. They do not say it in the next town over.

※

Her mother's calendar, her *lunario,* hung above the table on the kitchen wall, each day with its meteorologic prediction and the phase of the moon depicted in the lower right corner. The name of each day's saint. And on the page above, a Madonna and child. One month Bellini, one month Raphael, another month Giotto or Titian.

※

Attempts to order the days.

Calendar.

Almanac.

Appointment book. Feeble attempts.

Cancel all my appointments. I won't be in today.

※

Her mother developed an allergy to Latex gloves. She started wearing them in the first place because her daughter insisted.

Ma, do you know what they put into those cleansers?

Gloves slow me down when I work.

Letizia Mattei persisted. Then, you might as well soak your hands in a tubful of chemicals.

Fine, fine.

She wore them.

It was a rash on her skin that prompted her to see the doctor.

The cancer had nothing to do with the Latex gloves, though her mother believed that it did.

The arc of the disease was swift. Swifter than any stag.

To die of such a swift disease. Her knowledge of dendrites and axons, utterly, totally useless.

Drip. Drip.

Ma, you know . . .

I know, her mother said.

Letizia Mattei gripped the sleeve of the doctor. The crispness of the starched white cloth. She gripped his forearm through the cloth.

Fix her.

She is only sixty-two. Fix her.

My mouth is so dry.

Here Ma, do you want another piece of butterscotch?

Cancel all of my appointments for today.

※

The rash on my hands is gone, now get me out of here.

※

Cancel all of my appointments for the week.

※

Her mother was sitting on the sofa in the front room. It looked odd, her mother sitting in the middle of the sofa, in the middle of the afternoon. She was drinking lots of fruit juice, as the doctor had prescribed.

She said to her daughter, Go into the pantry and get down that jar on the top shelf.

Letizia Mattei went back into the kitchen, got the step-ladder and climbed up. She took down the jar and brought it to her mother.

When this is over, her mother said, take this jar to my mother's grave and spread all these pieces on the ground. That way there will be color, even in the winter.

But . . .

Don't argue with me, I'm too tired.

So Letizia Mattei has travelled here to sweep the pavement in front of the grave with an ancient broom and spread broken pieces of colored glass under the name of her grandmother.

※

All of the four walls of the cavern have now been lit. The wax of each candle drips. Drips.

Zacagnèr points outside the door, indicating the river.

242

Now, take this bucket and fill the basin in the middle of the floor with water.

She walks outside to the river. Snowflakes fall and melt on her exposed wrist. She knocks the edge of the bucket against the thin layer of ice and breaks it. She dips the bucket into the Scoltenna and the water is so cold her hand instantaneously numbs.

※

She pours water into the shallow basin in the center of the cave. Sunlight filters from two shafts and through the open door. Light emanates from candles. All of the light reflects in the pool, the rays break at the water, fragment, refract, then bounce back up to the dome's golden mosaic and illuminate the ultramarine. Broken light bounces off mirror shards embedded in the walls, in wings, in the eyes of hermit-saints, in the contents of the spilling ointment jar. Light bounces back down to the water, then up to halos and flames where ten angels wail in the midnight-blue sky, it refracts and bounces in all directions, and try as she might, Letizia Mattei cannot find a pattern. She stands among pathways of particles of light that reflect and bounce, seek out sites; it is not constant light, but light that flickers. She focuses on a single flame, its plump body with a tail rapidly unfurling outward in a hundred directions, and for one flicker-second, she stands inside synapse, the light from the flame spinning out threads to God-knows-where, to the next point of connection.

※

Far off, a bell lumbers, a low-tone, a slow knock.

It's getting late and I have a card game, Zacagnèr says. The others are waiting for me at the tavern, and I have the deck of cards.

The bell downstream in Ardonlà pounds six times.

It's time to go, he says.

Should I put out the candles? she says.

He looks at her, incredulous, offended, disbelieving.

You Americans . . . After all that climbing around . . . After light-
ing all those matches. . . .

For the love of God, he says in a gruff rasp. *Per l'amor d'Dio.* No.
Just leave them burning.

Grateful acknowledgment is made to the following publishers and publications where some of the stories first appeared: Guernica Editions, *The Voices We Carry*, Mary Jo Bona, ed. ("A Slight Blow to the Cheek"); Polyphony Press, *The Thing About Love Is . . .* , Mark Wukas, ed. ("With These New Tunes"); *River Oak Review* ("The Child Carrier"); *Santa Monica Review* ("The Coal Loader, Above Ground"); *Voices in Italian Americana* ("Waiting for Giotto"); White Eagle Coffee Store Press ("In the Gathering Woods," winner of the 1998 A. E. Coppard Prize for Long Fiction). The story "Waiting for Giotto" is the first chapter of Adria Bernardi's novel, *The Day Laid on the Altar,* winner of the 1999 Katharine Bakeless Nason Prize for Fiction, published by the University Press of New England in September 2000.

The translation of French troubadour poetry in the story "With These New Tunes" is from *Anthology of Troubadour Lyric Poetry*, Alan R. Press, ed. and trans., University of Edinburgh Press.